Rosey Thomas Palmer is a proud holder of dual nationality: British and Jamaican. She spread her work as an English teacher between these two contrasting islands. Since settling in Nottingham, though, she changed her career to health and social care, practising mainly in clients' own homes. This gave her access to interesting people and to in-depth local history. Along the way, these two passions have given rise to poetry, novels, plays and journalism. *Hues of Blackness: A Jamaican Saga* celebrates women, forthcoming *Coastal Turf* investigates men. *Lights at Sea* and, forthcoming, *The Candle Shop* examine migration. Meanwhile, contributions to Green Party publications honour the wonderful planet of which we are all a part, as poetry bubbles up from daily life in it.

Dedicated to all social care workers who have struggled through the 2020–21 pandemic to attend to clients of all ages and abilities. To all the companies, owners and directors who provide us with the opportunity to work in this industry and to the political activists who fight for due recognition of domiciliary health care staff. In particular, *Lights at Sea* is dedicated to all the brave and resourceful service users I have met who cannot be named or identified due to protective legislation.

Thanks to my editor and proof reader for remarkable patience and long faith in this book whilst personal challenges have come and gone.

Rosey Thomas Palmer

LIGHTS AT SEA

AUSTIN MACAULEY PUBLISHERS™

LONDON • CAMBRIDGE • NEW YORK • SHARJAH

A CIP catalogue record for this title is available from the British Library.

ISBN 9781398462212 (Paperback)
ISBN 9781398462229 (ePub e-book)

www.austinmacauley.com

First Published 2023
Austin Macauley Publishers Ltd®
1 Canada Square
Canary Wharf
London
E14 5AA

Research Sources

Greens of Colour, a sectional group of the Green Party of
England and Wales
Joy2care, my main care employer
Prestige, my first and most inspirational care employers

Writing Guidance

English teachers at Garrett Green School in the late sixties.
Sav Ink, a writers' co-operative in Jamaica in the eighties
and nineties
AM, my present publisher and their staff

Personal Encouragement

Hope Roberts, a health and well-being guide
Daughters, Xiomara and Annmarie
College friends, Carol and Mary.
Peter Pan, a childhood book that started my life's adventures

Table of Contents

Chapter One
Summer Lockdown

A multitasking mother of two, I felt I could only be grateful that I had spun them apart by the longest period available for safe births. Tanya, child of my teens, now a lanky and assured 21-year-old, was delving into imaginary futures as diverse as brewing craft beers and running a candle shop. Constance, born on the turn from my late thirties to forties, was a delightfully innocent six-year-old, still unaware that there were disadvantages in having an older, single mother. Yet, I vibrantly enjoyed my active lifestyle and gave a low-paid job my rapt attention. I was reassured by the picture-perfect town I had selected for our long-term home. Best of all, it was Hyacinth, their grandmother, and my mother-in-law, who had brought us here and who continued to hover around my concerns. I felt her supportive presence rather than relying on her help. She added to the cohesion of our small family unit.

"Miranda," she said many times, "you and your girls are the only close family I have, and I will face your problems as if they were my own."

Hyacinth lived not far up from the seafront in a modern complex for eldercare. Until seven years ago, I had lived in London.

"You need to stop trying to be a professional," she had told me firmly when I could no longer hide Constance's presence in my belly. "Give it up, sign on with a care company. Live in a better environment and use time more flexibly."

I was aghast and doubtful. Relinquish a solid income. Draw on a professional pension. Sell out a high-status property to a fifty-fifty division with Constance's dad and live off my own nerves and stamina?

"Do you really think it's wise to give up a steady wage and become part of the gig economy?" I felt both eager and nervous about sharing her vision.

"No," she would say. "Not all care companies offer zero hours. Some do a contract."

Eventually, she had won, and I had liberated myself from office work to sport a neat white uniform all over town, using corners and shortcuts to care for two widely spaced children.

It was summer in the seventh year after office work had ended for me. The amusement parks were again active after a break caused by government edict, and I looked forward to intervals in my rota when I would take two eager youngsters on the miniature village mile in the centre of town.

"You are much more of a child than you know, Miranda," Hyacinth had said, lovingly, when she saw my relish for the seaside and its activities. "It's a pity I still lived in the smoke near you when Tanya was six, otherwise I would have drawn you away to Southshire much sooner."

"But, if you had, I may not have given her a little sister," I had replied, gazing out to the blue horizon where the sea almost merged with the sky. "I think I came at exactly the right time to give Tanya a taste of freedom before whatever career she chooses closes in on her. At the same time, this allows Constance to grow with an older sister as her best friend and role model."

"Maybe, but don't expect too much of Tanya," Hyacinth had warned. "She will start to hanker after night-life, adult friendships, and, all too soon, there may be encounters in her love life that you would not choose. Try to look forward with her to lots of cheerful associations so that when she starts to look beyond our blue horizon, she will want to return to it again and again."

I had shivered, despite the sunlight, at my mother-in-law's predictions.

"Don't worry." Hyacinth had sensed my change of mood. "You have a few years of family completeness yet, and on the darkest nights, there are often lights at sea."

I had shaken those concerns out of my mind, replacing them with the promise of renewed summer enjoyments. I quickly consigned them to the back cupboards of memory, like unneeded winter wear, so that they did not darken the glint of the sun on the sea.

Now that Tanya was technically an adult, I caught myself wondering how soon those dark nights might draw in. That is how I characterised completely single parenting. Eventually, I would have to cope without the companionship of this child of my youth. Now she was practically a co-parent, but she was consciously choosing a different future.

"Oh look, Mummy, it's a white four-by-four like yours," cried Constance, jolting me back to the happier present by, pointing to a metre-high, hardened plastic replica of my own vehicle. It stood in an imaginative row of rocking vehicles, waiting to be operated through a slot machine.

Joyfully, I sat on it and hoisted her up in front of me, inserted coins, and moved the dummy gear stick into gear.

I felt the fairground device shoot backward.

"Mummy, you're facing the wrong way," cried Constance in alarm.

"She's not. She's just flung it into reverse," Tanya stated as she grabbed Constance, sliding her gently sideways to the safety of the firm ground.

"Why does it have two gears?" I exclaimed as I swizzled around, looking for a brake on the mini vehicle. "Yours has more than that," laughed Tanya, helping Constance to see the funny side of the incident.

The nodding heads of hibiscus in the hedgerows lining the amusement stand reflected the colour of my cheeks as I waited for the contraption's motion to stop before slinking back to my children.

"Okay, my time's gone," I resumed a coping tone as their giggles subsided. "Tanya will take you on the other rides," I told Constance.

Turning to my elder daughter, I said, "Hold on to the car keys for me in case you need anything out of it. I've only got an hour left to work."

Tanya opened her mouth to reply, but I decided to avoid any rejoinder about the driving lessons I could not afford to pay for or the CV she had planned to print. I hastily fixed my face mask. My mother-in-law and two of her neighbours in the complex were on my work rota. I patted my pockets, checking for PPE and sanitiser, and headed to Seaways Retirement Home. I was wondering how long our summer sunshine would safeguard our local health. The daily toll of hospitalisations and deaths was on the increase again.

Bulletins from across the country seemed to close in on us some days. By noon today, another set of government guidelines was expected.

My call to Hyacinth was to have her lunch. I said so, on entry, to the resident staff member who was delegated to check every visitor.

"Oh, fine," was the reply as they shot my temperature. "They are all in the lounge, at the moment, waiting for the announcement."

"Okay, I'll link up with Hyacinth there," I said.

The residents were sitting in an unusual line up of straight-backed chairs.

"The manager says we must all pay attention because restrictions will resume," muttered Hyacinth, gesturing me to an easy chair at the back. As I resigned myself to a few moments' wait, Hortense, my mother-in-law's neighbouring flat holder, whispered viciously, "They want to lock us up and incarcerate us before our time."

I held a professionally neutral expression over the flickering fears that my two calls would extend beyond an hour. My children might get bored, and the parking ticket would run out.

The government announcement, when it came, banned future use of the communal area and ordered all care home residents to self-isolate. Staff or visiting carers were to wear full PPE for every interaction, they said.

I put my apron and gloves on and slid my chair closer to the back wall as residents reached for their walking frames or beckoned carers to assist them into wheelchairs or hoists. Some angrily looked at me, wondering why a uniformed care worker was not rushing to their assistance.

The more agile pushed past me or stood in clusters commiserating with one another about the aloneness they would face.

I allowed time for the crush to clear. Some paused on their way out to collect small mementoes of their lives together to take back to their rooms.

Whilst Hortense, Hyacinth's neighbour, eagerly stripped photos from the display board, I noticed a framed medallion that honoured a craft initiative taken to its conclusion by Hyacinth. I took the medallion to her. She was eager to co-opt it and wanted a number of little keepsakes to add to it.

"Come over to this window," she indicated eagerly. "Here are some miniature lantern lights that reflect colours if they are turned at an angle. They will bend the light into my window just a little. I don't want any of the photos. I can still see my face in the mirror, but I am wearing a brooch in one of them. I need some feathers and dried flower heads to frame up in a similar design because I lost that one during the first lockdown."

Hyacinth moved like a magpie, busily from corner to corner of the lounge, collecting items to take to her room. I kept a wary eye on my watch and hovered, attempting to hold her trophies for her and to edge her towards the door. The time of my second call was approaching, I thought with alarm, and I could not begin the first yet, though I had been in the building for half an hour.

At length, we made it to Hyacinth's room, and I laid her treasures on the small windowsill over the main street. In the kitchenette, I microwaved her meal and served it precisely on her tray table with a clean napkin.

"I will go to Renee while you eat that," I said, "And wash up for you before I leave."

The company I worked for did not like us to double up in time this way, but this was one of those occasions when people could not be treated as automatons, besides which, my children were outside and would be wondering why I took so long.

Renee was further along the trajectory from independence to frailty than was Hyacinth. One of the staff had wheeled her to her room. She had been left with the brakes on her chair, waiting for me to assist her onto the commode. I did this and prepared her soup until she could be helped from the commode to her armchair. There she would drink the soup from a beaker. My main job was then to clean the commode and leave it ready for use when a carer returned with her tea. Renee would doze throughout the afternoon. I encouraged her to have as much of the soup as she could take, for she did not respond well to being left alone with it. I bit my lip and methodically made my notes before removing and rinsing her beaker.

To be back in Hyacinth's room was like breathing fresh air from a wide-open window. In her room, though, the window was narrow and opened onto the main road rather than facing the beach view. The corner of the sea from her window was just a turquoise triangle below a hard-boiled blue sky. The sea breeze slanted past her window without entering the room.

"How are your children?" Hyacinth asked.

"They are fine. They are down there waiting for me," I said.

"Oh, you should have brought them in today!" Hyacinth exclaimed.

"I can't bring them when I am officially working," I reminded her.

"But now I won't be able to see them at all," noted Hyacinth, sadly. "We are all to stay isolated in our rooms. Is that a life? Will you still come?"

"I will come as part of my job," I said. "As long as I wear this." I tugged at the mask and apron. "Now, let's set up your windowsill. To display your collection."

"No, it's alright, I'll do it; you go back to Tanya and Constance. I will show you what I've done when you come back."

I washed her plate, made a quick note, and left. My time showed an hour and three quarters since I had entered the complex.

Constance was fretful. Tanya was frazzled. It had been a long, hot wait on the city street. The parking ticket was fifteen minutes overdue. I rubbished it and shot off to a quieter zone along the coast road, thanking my stars for some small change that I could use to augment their sandwiches when I paused at a roadside fruit stall.

Constance whined as she exchanged a bedraggled sandwich for a fat slice of melon, "But Mummy, why didn't you take us upstairs to Hyacinth like you usually do?"

"This is not a usual time," I said, then sugared my statement by advising her to sink her teeth into the massive melon.

"But Constance is right, Mummy. You can't leave the child-care all on me."

"Why not?" I asked. "You are an adult, and you are her next of kin."

"But normally, I would be going off to university in a couple of weeks," reasoned Tanya.

"These times are not normal."

The severity of my assertion shook even me, and I gratefully handed a massive slice of melon to my right-hand woman. Whilst she sucked at its juicy pulp, I took advantage of her silence to try to focus her attention. "Hyacinth was not in her room. She was in a meeting in the lounge. I had to wait for her to finish. They are going into isolation. Everyone in the complex is to be confined to their rooms. Only care home staff and visiting carers will be allowed in for the foreseeable future."

"That stinks!" she said as she wiped her lips and discarded the melon rind. "Some of them already refer to the care home as being on death row."

"It's a hard pill to swallow but look how many of our elders lost their lives in the first wave of the pandemic. Do we want to lose Hyacinth early and avoidably?"

"Does she want to lose us and lose all other stimulation too?" snapped back Tanya.

I felt for her resistance and tried to soften the blow by saying that my career allowed me to go in, and I have designated Seaways calls so often that we would not lose contact.

Tanya shifted the grounds of her attack, "So you will keep on working like a mad thing, and I will continue to be an unpaid nanny?" she challenged.

"One of us receiving pay is better than neither of us," I said. "Do you know what it would be like to live on an isolation allowance? You could wish fresh fruit out of the window, and there'd be no petrol to drive us downtown, not even a rationale to be further out from home than a couple of kilometres."

In case Tanya wasn't convinced, I turned on the radio to the day's government briefing, so she could hear the latest panic in the administrative response.

"Oops," I said, "I forgot to check the evening schedule." Time check was followed by a quick reverse and a screeching park, not much further along than I had been that morning. "Use some of that money for some chips," I said. "I have three in here, then another break. Keep close to the car, and don't let Constance play where the other kids are."

I hastened back to Hyacinth, the first of three. She was standing at her narrow, corner facing window, squinting out at the triangle of beach that had been blue sea at midday. "The tide has moved out," she commented as I joined her. "I've never watched it continuously before. I was so eager to look at the full sweep to the sea front from the lounge. But, do you know, since you left and I've stood here to arrange these few bits and pieces, I've watched the colour change from blue to turquoise, then grey to brown, till it just looks like dull wetness."

I peered over her shoulder.

"Yes, it looks as if the tide has moved out a bit," I agreed.

"I so want to see the children," she said. "Don't you think they could stand just there, on the wet sand, and wave to me?"

"But for how long will you see them?" I wavered at the absurdity. "The tide will only allow you a glimpse just before sunset."

"It will vary a little from day to day," she persisted. "With changing tides, you wouldn't find it a heavy or repetitive task," she explained stoutly.

I reserved my objections and prepared her tea, wrote my notes and made my excuses to move on.

Renee was stiff, having sat in her chair too long. She did not feel ready for bed, she said, but I asked her to let me put her safely into it, as longer immobility would make the task even trickier later on and I didn't think the company would spare a second worker for a hoisted transfer. Renee's care was as complex as usual, but she knew me well and trusted me to support her weight when changing her clothes or pivoting her onto the bed once this was done. When we were through, I left her with fresh water in her beaker and pieces of fruit and chocolate to snack on.

Hortense was the most demanding of the three. She had the care to support her lifestyle rather than her health. Normally, she would have stayed in the lounge all day until her evening call, but today, she had been asked to go as soon as the meeting was over with the prospect of remaining in her room for the duration of the current wave of the pandemic. Her room was on the same side of the corridor as Hyacinth's, but it had a broad window parallel to the seafront instead of a corner one, where you could only just peek. She stood before the wide vista of the sea and sun, fretting about her glasses.

"I took the bifocals down with me, Miranda," she said. "But they have no shading. These distance ones shield me from the glare but distort the colours. I am sure I have some long-distance reactive lenses in my bedside drawer. Please find them for me."

I went to look and, returning with them, asked Hortense what she would like for tea.

"I haven't decided yet," she responded testily. "I need to ensure my view is precise and clear. How else can I accept day-to-day incarceration in this room?"

I looked around her apartment. It was, tastefully, furnished in light sea greens, the gloss painted skirtings and picture rails, an elegant grey. Her gauzy curtains were trained back and pooled to her steel grey carpet, and occasional lighting gave the room a calming glow adjustable to the sunrises and sunsets of the seascape.

"Oh, if my dear nephew were with me now!" she lamented. "He would have called the Home Office about this."

"About your glasses, don't they suit you?" I deliberately misinterpreted.

"No, about the curtailment of my liberties," she sighed. "You have nothing to complain about; you can come and go. We are the ones who are bearing the brunt of the infection."

"The isolation is an attempt to keep you safe," I assured her.

"And it may well do so as long as you bring nothing in to contaminate me," Hortense drifted to a chair and allowed me to tempt her to cake and cucumber sandwiches.

I made up her plate mindlessly and almost forgot to write my notes, finally turning to the records whilst the kettle boiled for her tea.

"What time will you be back?" she asked. "Don't come before ten. I cannot be expected to lie down too early at the height of summer."

She called me back as I was about to leave, wanting her fan plugged in and the window to be cracked open for the air. "Not so wide as to allow the street sounds in, though," she directed.

I breathed my re-found liberty as I followed the corridor out. I wanted to wash the work from my mind and snatch my few moments of undivided joy, reserving it only for myself and my girls but the image of Hyacinth, fingering a few baubles at a side window caught me up, and I decided to identify her triangle of wet sand before the late afternoon light drew in.

"Where are we going, Mum?" jibbed Tanya with uncharacteristic lassitude. I wondered if she was eager to be driven home and get Constance close enough to the bed to promise an evening of calls to friends of her own age. I glanced quickly in her direction but saw that her eyes looked heavy as if she craved sleep.

"We are finding the exact spot where Hyacinth can glimpse you," I said.

Hyacinth was Tanya's blood grandma, and they were fiercely loyal to each other, so Tanya held back her impatience to be home, and I hoped the breath of sea air would revive her.

It was Constance, who was sceptical, "How are you going to know she can see us?" she challenged when we stood in close arrow formation on the spot I identified.

"She will work out a way for next time if it doesn't work." I dodged her doubts. "I am sure she's looking. Just wave."

So, we stood and waved like three loonies in the lowering sun, with the wide expanses of beach on either side of us visible only to Hortense.

Chapter Two
The Triangle

My flat lay back from the popular area of the main street, just on the rise where fashionable downtown had given way to modest terraces. There, on a stray piece of unused land, some low-rise blocks had been built. They were intended to house local people who once had worked in the tourism sector and now found employment in retirement homes and care homes. Though I wasn't originally from the area, Hyacinth had thought ahead, and when her son had gone off to follow his army career, she had saved towards our purchase of the London council housing we occupied. My very young Tanya grew up in a London high-rise flat, but she had said, "You may not want to live in a big city all your life, Miranda. When I retire to the seaside, you could put your name down with a housing association nearby? You can explain to them that you are my only caregiver, and you will need to be near me in the future when I become less capable."

I had not thought that far ahead, and I still avoided the ominous prospect of Hyacinth's potential loss of capability. I was a conscientious young professional at the time, thinking that my interrupting marriage was just a blip in the inevitable upward movement of my life. A few forms establishing

Hyacinth as my future concern seemed no trouble to complete and of no immediate consequence to me.

She was satisfied. She folded the papers neatly together in an envelope and told me to write the address while she searched for a stamp. I was surprised when Hyacinth did not return the envelope to me for posting.

"No, that's fine. I'll drop it when I go to draw my pension," she said.

Remembering her lingering smile, now, I realised the depth of my mother-in-law's love and her extreme patience throughout those years when I had battled with youthful expectations of excelling as a working mother with a top-flight career.

Refocusing on the present, I let myself into the flat. It was ground floor, opening from a little entry garden so that, once inside, you forgot it was a part of a block, and it felt like a seaside cottage that you could rent for a couple of weeks of rare freedom. The open-plan lounge was high-ceilinged and airy, allowing for stairs to a mezzanine gallery, where there were two-bedroom bays. A larger bedroom opened from one side of the lounge downstairs, the bathroom from the other side. The kitchen lined the back wall of the living space, divided from it by my auction-acquired deal table.

Tanya went straight upstairs and stayed in her bedroom while I prepared Constance for bed. I sat her on the long green settee to watch children's television and turned to the kitchen to fix her supper. When I looked up, the channel was flicking diagonally across the screen, complaining, voicelessly, that she had not pressed the continuation button. Both my girls seemed to be exhausted, I concluded, retrieving the remote from a limp childish hand and noting the length of time that had passed since Tanya disappeared upstairs.

I roused Constance to eat a little, then cleared the toys from her bed and led her to it. Constance's struggle to remove her skew-whiff dressing gown finally exhausted her. I eased it off and wrapped its loose end around her two favourite dolls, where they lay on the floor beside her bed. I pulled up the door in case we should become noisy and went to the kitchen to prepare food for myself and Tanya.

Tuna on toast, gherkins, and beetroot and two mugs of cocoa were piled on a tray which I carried carefully upstairs. I nudged Tanya with my foot whilst I looked for somewhere to rest it. She woke with a jerk. "Oh, Mum, what time is it?" she asked.

"Nearly time for me to go back to work," I said. "Let's have this together before I go."

"Oh, Mum, can I have mine later? I really don't feel hungry."

"Okay, I will stay with you a bit, and I won't be out for long. You must have used all your energy with Constance. She was tired too."

"Is she in bed now?" Tanya checked.

I assured her that she was and encouraged her to eat the food once she was fully awake. Tanya argued about the time when I told her I thought it was after nine.

"You are so unspecific," she complained. "There's a movie I want to watch."

She stood to go downstairs and seemed to stagger a bit. She reached for her blanket, shivering as she pulled it close around her. When I followed her downstairs. She reached for the remote and trained it on the television, bringing up some weird music and the shadowy image of a voluptuous female.

"Okay," I said, "why not eat then do your teeth and change for bed before you watch it?"

"No, later," Tanya insisted, cuddling into the settee. "It's too cold to move now."

"Shall I fetch the tray for you?"

"Oh, Mum, go off to work. They don't like it if you are late."

I went, still puzzling about Tanya's exhaustion, but my gratitude to her for hastening me increased when Hortense's opening gambit was, "Why were you standing out there with that woman and a child, waving, after you left me at tea-time?"

"That wasn't a woman; that was my daughter, and the child was my other daughter," I amazed myself by defensively allowing a chink of my real existence into my working life.

"Oh, and were you waving to me?" Hortense's tone suggested a lack of social distance on my part.

"No," I said, hastening to deny an intrusion. "I was waving to someone around the corner."

The call continued as a curious dance, verbally performed, to probe and recoil as Hortense tried to follow up on my disclosure, and I tried to avoid it. "Though you may be settling me in now, I am often restless at various times in the night," Hortense spoke as if she were delivering a warning. "There isn't much that goes on out there that I don't know about." Her eyes narrowed, and she tapped her aquiline nose. "These eyes see more than this mouth says," she promised with a knowing look.

By the time I reached Hyacinth's flat, she had got herself into bed. She did not require the extra pampering that went with my attendance on Hortense. I was eager to know if she had seen us, but I needed to wait until morning for that because she slept lightly and did not benefit from excitement late at night.

Grateful for the forethought of settling Renee to bed early, I nipped and checked that she was comfortably slumbering, filled in her notes under a dim side lamp, switched it off, and went home.

Tanya had taken her time but was on her way to the bathroom when I climbed our mezzanine stairs to the space that passed for a master bedroom. I was out like a light and woke with the dawn to an empty front room, a sink full of dishes, and an urgent need to iron a uniform. Constance was beginning to stir, so I whispered to her to play quietly in her room, gave her juice, toast, and cereal, and went out.

It was a crisp, clear summer morning. Birds twittered in the silver birch by my gate. They had marked my car, but I'd go to the car wash in my break. I drove fast to the complex to get Hortense up. She had forty-five minutes for a shower, assisted dress, and continental breakfast. Today she decided to wash her hair. I tried to calculate the best way to multi-task so the call would not run too long over. I slipped out quickly, leaving some tendrils to dry on her nape as she sat facing the silver vista of the morning sea.

Hyacinth had been up early. She only washed her face and hands if she got to it before I came. I made a note to insist on a proper wash later. She was bursting with plans, though.

"I saw you wave last night," she said. "The sun was really low. Can you go back half an hour earlier tonight? I want to see if the sun's rays will refract through these lantern lights I brought up to make a point of light reach where you are."

I was cautious. "Remember, that's the time I should be with Hortense," I said.

"How about Renee, could you go to her earlier and take a break before Hortense?"

"You'll get me into trouble," I chided.

"Well, but I really want to try to reach someone out there," she pressed.

"Reach someone?" I asked.

"Yes, be able to send a Morse-coded message like we used to do when I was a child," she insisted.

I decided ingenuity was required here so I said, "I will ask Tanya to be there for a long enough time to test out your messaging. Most people use their mobiles and have a chat, or text these days."

"I know they do, but that's not environmental, is it? The essence of life is three-way, you know!"

"I know," I said, remembering the pep talks with which she upheld her vision of me moving to the coast. "You always told me I was too cut off from reality when I worked in an office and travelled there by tube."

"Yes, you only did just make it in time. If you had followed Tanya's choices, you'd be there in the city to this day. Even when I had sorted out your prospects, you still had to delay it all by entangling with Constance's dad."

The assault was a little raw for me at this time of the morning. I frowned with concentration on her notes, parcelled out the medications and slammed down water, and perked coffee in an attempt to remove myself from her revived impatience with me.

"Nut Clusters or cornflakes?" I sang out after writing ubiquitous 'cereal', adding milk to a dish, and putting the chosen packet beside it. "Later! I'll do what I can about the beach. If you don't see me there, it will be the girls, depending on how I can flex the time."

Renee's call was not for another half an hour. I got back to my flat to check on Constance since Tanya hadn't been seen earlier that morning. A trail of spilled milk led from the side bedroom to the settee where Constance was curled up with a chocolate lollipop. "Did you have your juice?" I asked.

She regarded me with big solemn eyes and nodded slowly. "Melanie's mum takes her shopping on Saturdays," she said, with a hint of accusation.

"Not now. This is Covid time," I answered firmly, "Supermarkets don't like children, and there's an alarming report about people getting infected when they go shopping. Later on, Hyacinth is going to make some pretty lights blink at you when you go down to the beach. You and Tanya can have fun. Tell her to find some little mirrors to take. You might be able to blink back."

Secure in the fact that I had been environmental enough to please even Hyacinth, I went back to the car and whizzed around to Renee.

This was the one to whom I had to go with a quiet mind. She was stiff, wet, and sore. I peeled off her pad while she still lay on her side. I washed, dried, and creamed her buttocks on that side, then pulled out her bed and rolled her over to do the other side. She was grateful and trusting as usual and woke up enough to sit firmly on the bed and pull herself up for me to position a fresh daytime pad. She transferred to the closed commode seat for me to give her a wash and dress her top half.

"Remember, you are not going to the lounge today," I prompted softly. "Everyone has to stay in their rooms now. It is part of the government's precautions."

She didn't seem to be able to take it in, but she complied when I wheeled the commode seat to the comfy chair in the corner. She slid into it, and I wedged the pillows around her. I went to the communal kitchen and collected porridge for her, then made the tea to go with it in her room.

"Do you want the television on?" I asked, hoping the news would not be too bad. She nodded wordlessly.

Notes, MAR sheet, medication, all was done, yet she looked wistful and abandoned.

"I'll be back at lunchtime," I promised.

My girls were both dressed. All credit to Tanya, there were no more trails of milk. Beds were straightened, toys piled up, used dishes in a neat stack in the washing-up bowl, toothpaste sealed, and enough blue smudges around the basin to show they had been used.

Tanya's hair was tumbled lightly around her shoulders, and Constance's was being combed in a smooth plait down the back of her head.

"My day," said Tanya. "How much time do I have?"

"The rest of the morning," I offered, hoping she wouldn't jib.

"That's only half," she announced. "I'll be back for the rest."

"Okay," I shrugged to keep it casual, "be back by twelve."

I turned my attention to Constance. "Home schooling," I said firmly.

"But, Mummy, it's Saturday. People don't home school on Saturdays.

"They do when their mothers worked too many hours in the week," I assured her.

"Oh, bother!" resented Constance.

"Come and read your book," I coaxed.

"Not, that one, not that one." Constance screwed her face at the standard text, whipped around, and grasped two alternative titles from her own shelf.

"Okay," I said brightly. "Some of each."

We started with her favourite and then searched for words read there in the school text. This made the reading a treasure adventure, and the second book of her choice was an easy romp of waves on a seashore, rolling stones to soft gleaming roundness, and offering sea minnows to nibble children's toes.

"Number," I said.

"No," she said.

"How many apples for each of us to have one?"

"Three, easy-peasy."

"How many, if two?"

So, the game went on till there were fewer and they needed cutting. Then, half an hour earlier than agreed, Tanya came home.

She was crestfallen. She had a crushed copy of her CV in her hand.

"The craft beer places have all had to close. The regular pubs can't serve their food, and the cafés can only serve people in queues outside," she grumbled. "So, this isn't worth the paper it's printed on," she said, flinging it in the bin.

"So, what about the job in the candle shop," I asked.

"They are closed too. Non-essential items," clipped Tanya.

"Oh, so you can just start up your own outlet, then, can you?"

"Only online. I could do it online, I suppose."

I knew nothing of the technicalities of online businesses, but I supposed it was possible if people were inclined that way. I felt a kind of distanced respect for the woman my daughter was becoming. This aspect of her was one I did not know. I knew her to be petulant, reluctant, resentful of the role she played as 'unpaid nanny' to our threesome, but I did not know the remote pride of her forward looking to a life lived beyond mine.

"Your time to go to work," she said abruptly.

"Are we going to the beach this afternoon, Tanya?" wheedled Constance.

"After lunch. I haven't had any breakfast this morning," was Tanya's response.

I suddenly realised I hadn't either, as I had rushed home instead of taking the car to the car wash.

Right after the lunch calls, I will sort something out, I thought. If my girls could occupy each other, I could use my afternoon break for myself.

"Can you meet me at the beach right after the tea calls?" I asked. "There's something I want to show you."

"Mummy has a plan," proudly confided Constance. "She wants us to take some bits of a mirror with us."

"Oh, I have a compact somewhere," exclaimed Tanya.

"And I have a mirror that came with my mermaid doll," offered Constance.

I was content. They would spend the afternoon unearthing these treasures, and I would have a mid-afternoon break to myself.

An hour or so later, I drove eagerly, armed with an orange juice and a flapjack, into the car wash. No one could imagine the delicious privacy of those mechanical walls and lower cascades. Isolated by smoothly enveloping roller-mops, I enjoyed total submergence to resurface, gleam clean, with little runnels of water like the dew of the dawn, finding ways to re-join the sunlight. Those I cared for did not have this option of escape and renewal. They were locked in by decisions made earlier in their lives, obliged to tread alleyways of imposed security laid down by advisors who concentrated on the slow deterioration of age that they saw as the modern norm.

I drove down to the seafront again and identified the precise spot that was Hyacinth's triangular view of a wet strip of sand. With luck, I would finish my three calls before the low rays of evening sun faded too far for her to try its glinting refraction.

I parked higher up, nearer to Seaways Care Home, brushed oat crumbs from my uniform, and went to Hortense's flat.

She swung around from the window in sudden agitation as I entered. "There's a green light out there, far to sea."

She spoke as if I were responsible for the unexplained appearance of this phenomenon.

"Out where?" I asked, squinting at the bright blue horizon. "Are you sure it's not just the glare? Do you want to put on your shades?"

"I told you, my long sight is perfect," she said, drawing herself up to a regal height and looking down her long nose at me. "There is a vessel or a platform out there that has never been there before, and it is hovering on the horizon."

"I don't know anything of it," I said, inexplicably feeling that I had to deny all knowledge to assert a feeble hold on my own innocence. "Perhaps my daughter, Tanya, will be able to see it when we go out later. I'll ask her to look."

I quietly shelved a warrant of guilty quickly delivered to me in the parent role. Had I really implicated my fresh, disingenuous daughter in the rambling imaginings of an elderly woman doomed to remain cooped up too long?

Routine was the only safe refuge from such morose meanderings of the mind, so I quickly emptied the teatime medication from her blister pack and gave them to her with water, bending over the Mar chart to complete it.

"What can I get you for tea?" I asked.

A recitation of what was in the fridge would have to be avoided, I decided, so I opened it and sang the praises of an avocado pear so effectively that she accepted it with a scone and butter without time-consuming indecision. Notes done, tea made, and Hortense comfortably, if briefly, seated. I went on to Renee.

I had left her out of bed at lunchtime, but now she needed the commode and was not inclined to go back in as early as she had the previous night. I could not rush her. The call exceeded my time. She needed careful skincare as she was too weak to reposition herself much. I needed to push fluids for a diet of soup and porridge did make her very thirsty, and she liked warm but not cold water. I had to persist in getting her to drink a full cup before I left, knowing that she would leave it if it got too cold.

"Don't leave me very late, will you, Miranda?" she asked.

"I'll do my best." I avoided making too much of a commitment as I needed to have my own time for a little that night.

Speedily to Hyacinth's, I nearly stumbled on the stairs. She was prepared at her side window with her paraphernalia.

"You will be sure to be out there tonight, won't you," her tone betrayed the anxiety of the isolated. "I will be able to make out with the girls before sunset falls. You have timed it well enough, haven't you?"

I did all the official tasks of my visit at the speed of lightning. I felt it was so much more important to give her a glimpse of her granddaughters, but the notes, the MAR Sheet, and the tea, were what gave me the rationale to remain in her life on a regular basis. I wanted to bend and kiss her as I left, but I couldn't. I backed away to maintain my distance and waved goodbye from the door. "Watch us from the window," I called airily, as if it was not a carefully choreographed encounter along a limited strip of time. I went to the car, my heart skipping ahead to see if my girls were there, waiting.

Tanya's long tumbling hair was touching the top of Constance's neatly plaited head as she bent to point my urgent approach out to her.

"Mummy, I've got lots of mirrors," Constance rushed eagerly as she spread her hands to show stickily clutched reflective pieces.

"Okay, don't drop them," Tanya reprimanded and swooped to retrieve two that tinkled to the ground. "Mummy wants them in the car, not scattered all over the street."

"Yep, let's get in and get down to the water," I said, throwing Tanya a grateful look that would cost me privileges later.

Down we drove. My fears about being unable to park near the designated spot were unfounded. We got out and moved to the target area that could be seen from Hyacinth's window. The lowering sun shone in a direct line, up past the flat of Seaways building, to the sill that opened into her room. The window was lifted and there, below the slanting pane, was a fragile hand holding a coloured lantern glass. The dying sunlight winked blue at us, and Tanya drew a doll's mirror from Constance's collection to bounce the light back up the street. It missed the window, but another light called back to it, a bright, ruby red that Tanya caught in a compact mirror and bounced accurately back to the open windowsill. We were ecstatic, laughing, confident. Constance jumped and waved, star-shaped, to kiss fingertips in the direction of the light. Tanya stood solemn and intent, carefully firing back light-signals to her marooned grandma. My heart swelled with pride to have two girls so joyous in overcoming a harsh curtailment of natural interaction. The light was gone, all too soon. It fell to a greyish amber line that dipped below the horizon and mingled with the sand of the seabed.

"Can we do it often, Mommy? Can we come again tomorrow?"

I did not want to promise or deny it. I did not know how often we could replicate that exact timing. "We'll see," I said. "I'll come home and cook for us before I go back to work."

Tanya saw her moment. "Mummy, can I follow you home?" she asked. "I'm not hungry yet. I'll be back by six-thirty."

I could not refuse. She had spent the whole day enabling this little scheme to keep Hyacinth connected.

Chapter Three
Green Light

"I told you there was a green light out there," Hortense rounded on me as I entered her room. "I told you, but you with your fool-hardy ways took your children out there again and stood out on the sand, attracting them in." Her eye's flashed and her finely waved hair seemed to stand higher from her head as she added to the catalogue of my carelessness. "You even left that long lanky girl of yours on the shore alone. For what? To come here. What have you done with the smaller one? Not left her alone at home, have you?"

I knew it was not wise to let the clients have any knowledge of our lives, but here I was, caught in a small seaside town where everyone's business was fair game, and no one's life was sacrosanct.

"Tanya came home before I left for work," I said calmly.

"Yes, but not before she'd stood on the beach like a Disney mermaid, waiting and watching as the green light came nearer and nearer." Hortense's voice almost jeered over me, a careless outcast from status and privacy. Guilty of my choice of a caring career, and guilty of my alacrity in doing it. I said little throughout the call. I prepared everything for her comfort and convenience and kept my eyes averted from the window and the light that may have been playing there.

Renee pulled at my heartstrings as usual. She had lost the pluck that had made her stay in her chair, she needed no more cleansing or changing, but she was very weak and clung pitifully to me during the transfers from chair to commode seat, from there to bed, and away from the edge into a comfortable, protective groove of pillows.

"You may need the alarm for the night staff," I reminded her, putting it close to her hand. "Don't hesitate if you need to use it. You are paying for that option," I reminded her.

It was a relief to go to Hyacinth. The level of her anxiety had dropped, reassured by her pride in her granddaughter's growth and potential. Although I encouraged both my daughters to see her in the same role, her pride in her true descendant was evident and heart-warming. "She is so tall and slim and upright. She reminds me of her grandfather's side of the family and my poor son, Algie."

Hyacinth didn't often mention my first husband. He could have left the army after our marriage, and once I knew I was pregnant, I urged him to do so, but he was caught up in the excitement of it.

"Just one more tour of duty," he would say, one hand in mine and one where Tanya lay in my belly. "Then I'll come back to you, I promise you." I turned my mind to preparing the flat, making a little nursery out of the box room and papering the bedroom walls with jungle print so he would not feel too shut in by high town walls.

But he stepped on a mine, they said.

One whoosh and he was gone.

They even thought they were consoling me by assuring me that he would never have taken to civilian life.

"Though you may be settling me in now, I am often restless at various times in the night." Hortense spoke as if she were delivering a warning. "There isn't much that goes on out there that I don't know about." Her eyes narrowed, and she tapped her aquiline nose. "These eyes see more than this mouth says," she promised with a knowing look,

Hyacinth had not tried to console me. She was as open with her anger and her pain as I was. There were times when we raged at each other until we cried torrents. The only time Hyacinth's sense of loss stemmed was when she held the baby Tanya in her arms and crooned lullabies she had used for her son.

Those were strange pent-up days. I worked in an office downtown. She visited for half the week to help with childcare costs. I was shut into myself except for Friday nights when lack of work the next day opened the lock gate on the sorrows and fears of lone parenting, and she regarded me with a sense of exhaustion, eager to go to her own home, maybe to pretend to herself that he was still alive somewhere.

Hyacinth kept up her availability until Tanya was thirteen. Then she found the sharp brashness of the teen years too hard to take.

"I don't want to reopen old wounds," she told me gently and firmly. "I have to put in a bit of distance. Don't wrong me, my dear, I will always be there for you, but you need space to get over it too. Maybe you should marry again. You didn't get much of him, did you?"

She faded away. She kept the Christmas and birthday presents coming, but her letters were few and brief. She did not believe in mobile phones, and she had that old-fashioned reserve about phone calls that predated family and friends deals.

I tried to take her advice. Tanya was old enough to have sleepovers with school friends, and she was a friendly, popular girl. My married female friends and those who were hooked up thought they could spot promising partners for me. Sometimes they introduced us. Sometimes they co-dated. Some lesbian women suggested the same-sex solution. I could have tried, but I still felt for men.

He was very plausible. A man from Algie's unit, he was shocked, he said, by the senseless loss of life. Pensioned out very soon because of shell shock, he had staggered along through life for twelve years till he met me. He said he felt like Tanya's second dad, someone Algie had sent to look after her. He interfered with her. I ran and told Hyacinth. That was when she moved us out.

"There's a ground floor flat inland from Seaways," she said. "It would be in your price range. We have saved enough between us now."

I was a bit of a magpie, bolstered by beautiful things in my flat, but also secured by carefully hoarded savings.

"You can't take it with you when you go," she said. "Use it to give Tanya a better start in life."

I resisted her, fending off Darfield with one hand and structuring safety around my daughter with the other. I encouraged her to stay away from him with friends in the suburbs, under-estimating how much I would miss her and how easily I would fall prey to him again in my lonely state.

When I went to Hyacinth to tell her I was pregnant, she took me again to view the flat.

42

"Now, you have no excuse," she said.

"But I won't be able to work," I said. "I can't commute that far, and I'll have a baby to look after."

Hyacinth looked at me hard, almost saying, "Again."

Yet she resisted provocation and calmly said, "You can be a carer. People employ them all the time at Seaways."

So, she decided for me, spoke to the estate agent, paid a deposit, "Out of Algie's childhood savings," she said. She identified a couple of care companies, booked interviews for me, and looked after Tanya while I was interviewed. I could not understand why they were hiring a pregnant woman, but Hyacinth knew.

"They'll be very glad of you," she said. "Most of their workers are school-leavers or migrants. Either way, they're on their way up to London, where wages are higher, and opportunities are greater. Whichever company you choose can train you and take you through probation before maternity leave starts. When you are ready to go back, I'll help out a bit."

So, I did as she said, and soon Darfield was a bad memory erased by sun, sea, and sand and an airy, elegant flat with a little front garden into which we all welcomed Constance and named her for the quality we were determined to add to our lives.

Chapter Four
From the Hills

It took me years to understand how much Hyacinth valued stability. Her determination to add this to my life drew us closer to each other after Algie's death. When I was distracted by loneliness and drained by new motherhood, Hyacinth came and sat with me. To distract me, she began to describe her childhood home.

"It was away up in the hills," she would say. "So far on a winding road, you couldn't go up there. We had donkeys, but that was just to help with the load. Mostly we would walk and carry produce on our heads. Coming down was long swaying strides. Coming back was a slow uphill trudge with the goods we had bought to keep us going for the next week."

"I was younger than your Tanya when I started in the market. My mother died, you see, and I was left with my dad, who worked the land, and two smaller children who were just babies. It was my job to go to market on a Friday morning and return on Saturday evening. Sunday was Church for my father was a strict man, and Monday to Thursday, I could go to school if my brother and sister were well."

Hyacinth smiled as she told the tale and demonstrated, with raised, cupped hands, how the cocoa pods hung low over the house, how she could lean from the veranda to pick them and let them dry to grating goodness on a zinc sheet in the corner of the veranda. "Chock-let tea, we called it, it was thick and sweet and creamed with coconut milk."

She would lick her lips in memory, and I would offer her a coffee. Then she would resume. "Well, I got pregnant, you see, for a young man living near me. When my father found out, he sent me away to hide my shame. I spent two nights under the house-bottom because it was raised on stones at the edge of the hillside. Then I banded my belly tight and went down to my auntie in the town. I lived with her like a country cousin, helping her in every way I could until she could not mistake my condition. Up, I was sent again to the country district to make what shift I could."

"Well, there was an older man there who wanted a housekeeper, so I lived with him, and he let me keep my child after birth, but there was no affection there. I appealed to my cousin in England to send for me and let me live with her. She was not ready for it; she was still living in a multi-occupation house, and there was no spare room. Eventually, my young man, Algie's father, went up and was able to send for me, but he married to someone else when I was on the way coming."

Hyacinth's round-cheeked cheerfulness had never betrayed the upheavals she recounted while sitting on my green settee in a newly adopted home. I took pride in her and received her story as my challenge. If she had made a life of contentment and stability, so could I.

"How did you manage with a young baby on your own?" I asked.

"He was school age at the time, and his teacher loved him, so she took him into her home and promised to keep him until I could send the fare."

"So, you came up without him?" I prompted.

"Yes, it was a wrench, but if you want better, your nose must run," smiled Hyacinth. "I came, and I made my way. That's why I know you can do it too. I promise to help. I will do a bit of babysitting for you, and you go and arrange your hours with that company so that you can come and go, and it won't be too much burden on me."

So, there it was. I learned to accept my single state with pride. I made my flat a home. I had a job and a mother-in-law, and I recited my gratitude, quoting a song she often sang while she helped me settle in: "This is the day the Lord has made. Let me rejoice and be glad in it."

My reverie had lasted too long. I caught myself from it. Supper plates were on the floor by my feet. Constance had crept into her own room and fallen asleep playing with her dolls on the bed. Tanya was not here yet, and my time to return to work was just a few minutes away. I washed the dishes and warmed Tanya's food at the same time. I sent a quick text telling her the food was hot. I washed my face to banish the traces of memory lane. I waited, impatient, by the garden gate.

Tanya seemed flushed and hurried.

"You almost missed the time," I said, but she offered no explanation. She just smiled, and I left.

"I told you not to let your girl linger out there!" Hortense raged. "I watch all the boats coming in. I see them all. Look at that green light which you couldn't see."

I stood beside her and peered out into the gloom. I could see no light below the horizon, but I did make out a small, dark shadow against the waves.

"It's a boat. It's coming to land," Hortense insisted.

"Are you ready to change for bed?" I asked, focusing on things I could cope with.

"Yes, I need a wash, my feet too. I need the chiropodist."

"I can wash and cream your feet," I agreed, "but no occasional workers are allowed into the building at present."

"And I can't go out," said Hortense, aggrieved. "At least I have a wide window to observe what is going on, not like your mother-in-law." She looked at me piercingly as she made the comparison. "What were those antics all about, flashing lights earlier on? Is it you who was beckoning the boat in?"

"Me? I was only looking at the sea with my children."

"Yes, and leaving one there to look more and more."

"She is safely at home now with my younger daughter."

"You hope she'll stay there, don't you?" she said with the spite of a childless woman. "That boat's coming in. She called it in."

I was perplexed by her weaving of popular topics into my life. Hortense was fascinated by local television news, and she was always applying new items to her observations from her window. When a white vehicle was implicated in a recent abduction, it was my vehicle parked within her sight that contained the lost child. When day visitors trashed the promenade, she was sure she had seen Tanya prominent in the group. When a child fell at the amusement park and was hospitalised, I was guilty of allowing my little one to take a similar risk.

At times like these, I took refuge in silence and routine, but it was difficult when she spun out the time of a call as she was doing today. I needed to get away before my professional control broke.

"I'll get into bed later, on my own," Hortense said when she realised I was not going to open up. "I will finish my observations first."

I breathed deeply at the exit to clear the stress building up in me. Renee was a joy. I cared for her meticulously and edged her comfortably into bed. I did not need to go back to Hyacinth for work purposes, but my feet lingered at her door. She looked around when I peeped in.

"Going back to your babies?" she said.

I nodded.

"Remember, Tanya is almost a woman now. You'll have to get used to that."

My impulse was to tell her about the job disappointment at the craft beer bars and the candle shop, but time was against me, and, overcomer as she was, she would only start telling me to encourage Tanya to make candles at home and sell them online. I didn't know if I could put up with the mess and the smell in my flat.

I smiled, told her we loved her, and went home.

Which lady was the prophetess or whether they were equally sighted, one for doom and one for the boon? I don't know. I only know my breath caught short when Tanya sidled past me at the door and said, "I'll soon be back."

The front garden was cool dark blue velvet, and the stars twinkled brighter than any gleam at sea, but she was gone out of sight in an instant, and I had no view, where I lived, of the long sweep of the beach or the waves rippling from far away forward. I wanted to call Hyacinth and ask her to watch out of her window, but it was a side view of just a darkened slot of the sea. I would have had to call Hortense for ongoing information, but I could not shame myself and my daughter that way.

If I walked up away from the town to the foothills of the downs, and then up the sharp slope beyond the cemetery, I would have a wider vista of the sea than Hortense through her window. Constance was here, though, sleeping, and my calls began early the next morning. I started to write a note to leave on the kitchen table, then realised this could not hasten Tanya home, so I texted her phone. My message rambled a bit about my need for an early night and the key concealed under a garden stone. Two parental texts on one evening were crowding a bit, I thought, but guilt looked at me through Hortense's remembered eyes, so I clicked send and put the key under the stone, clicking the self-locking main door closed firmly.

I went through compulsory pre-bed rituals and stretched myself with determination across my bed on the mezzanine. A mosquito whirred in my ear. I shook my head to cover my face with hair, and gently plumped up the pillow. My limbs stretched, relaxed, stretched again. My head grew fuzzy with sleep. I heard a key click in the lock. The door opened and closed. I, being sleep-drugged, struggled to surface and call Tanya's name, but slumber covered my brain like a welcome blanket until I woke with a start in the thin light of dawn and rushed to the door. It clicked open. The key lay on top of the concealing stone.

I staggered back inside, mounted the mezzanine again, and peeped into Tanya's side of it. The bed was undisturbed.

My semi-sleep nightmare cleared to total alarm. I was awake, carrying a stone of fear somewhere in my gut. I called Constance's name sharply and dressed her in leggings and sweaters.

"Where are we going?" she asked.

"For a walk," I said.

Programmed by my patterning of Hortense the night before, I strode up the road with Constance in her old buggy, ignoring her protestations of, "Mummy, I'm six now."

I ditched the buggy in a bush, where the road petered out just past the cemetery and restored her dignity by demanding that she kept up with me on the foot-worn path between bushes and below trees to the top-most vista of the downs. I rushed out seawards and scanned the waves in detailed concentration, looking for a boat, a light, a platform. Even a person swimming, dipping, and rising over the coast-ward waves would have heartened me; nothing, no one. I had to retrace my steps, calm down, make a plan, and cry off work. What does one do when one's child does not come home? Or comes and doesn't stay?

This time, Constance was not above the push chair. She stretched her aching limbs across the foot plate. I wheeled like the wind, spun at the gate, and stopped with a jerk at our front door. It was locked, and the key was not on the stone.

"Where is she?" I wailed. "Has she taken the key? Is she inside?"

"Mummy, I can find out," volunteered Constance.

"How can you find out?"

"I can climb in the window," she said, pointing up at my mezzanine. It was open.

"How can you get up there?" I asked.

"It's not as high as Melanie's, she is my best-est friend, and she lives in a two-storey house. She can get in the upstairs window. Mummy. Let me! I can help."

"How will you get up to that window?" I breathed in awe of her courage.

"You will lift me up, Mummy. I will stand on your shoulders."

I positioned myself directly under the window, facing the wall, then crouched, so she could climb piggyback and then hump up to my shoulders. From there, she sat, then stood, my raised hands cupping hers to steady her.

"One hand at a time," I warned her shakily under the pressure of fear and her weight.

"Yep," she said sturdily, releasing one of my hands to grip the window ledge. She tried the other hand but, lacking leverage, she grabbed back at my hand and instructed me to guide her foot up.

Adult hesitation was ruled out under the impetus of an intent child, so I did as she said and raised her foot high enough for her to kneel on the window ledge. In no time, she was thorough, and I collapsed, a shivering mass of nerves, on the doorstep, while she skimmed the stairs, crossed the room and flung wide the door.

"Now, Mummy," she took charge. "Get ready for work and put on your uniform. You can go to Know-it-all-Hortense, and she can tell you what happened to Tanya last night."

"Where will you go if I go to work now?"

"I'll go to Hyacinth," she said.

"You can't. It's a lockdown. You have to stay with your own family."

"Well, then I'll sit in the car. You would let me if Tanya were with me, so I will sit still and keep my head down. No one will know I'm there."

Decisiveness is a winning quality, no matter the age of who expresses it.

I did as I was told while Constance helped herself to cereal and juice and set a bowl for me on the kitchen table too.

Chapter Five
The Sea Front

I trembled as I walked into Seaways that morning. I knew the next call would be the police if I did not find my daughter by this means. My attitude to Hortense was different. Although she was provocative and inquisitive, I knew I was reliant on her observation and wished I had taken her hints more seriously. She seemed reluctant to open the conversation that morning.

I prompted her, "That boat you saw, did you see it come closer?"

"I lost interest in it when you left here," she tried.

"So, you don't know if the green light stayed on out at sea all night?"

"What time did your daughter come home? You could ask her if it was still on then."

I knew she had put me on the spot, and I could not afford to pursue this, although, my eyes were welling up, and I had a mounting sense of panic about Constance sitting in the car. I was literally flinching at the thought of another vehicle missing its distance as it tried to pass my parked car, damaging it to the point of injury. I left hastily when the call was over, not remembering that although the MAR sheet was completed, I had not written the daily log.

I avoided Renee's and went straight to the car to get Constance out.

"I didn't stand up, Mummy; I did keep down."

"I know, Constance, Hyacinth wants to see you," I said.

I took her straight to my mother-in-law's flat.

"Oh, dear," she said, understanding straight away. "Where is Tanya?"

I crumbled, "I don't know," I sobbed. "She didn't come in last night."

"You can't work like this," Hyacinth decided. "You need time to sort this out."

"They won't have anyone else to send for my calls," I cried. "The company won't let me stop."

"Do you have anyone else to go to now?" Hyacinth asked. She welcomed Constance and sent me off to Renee, saying she would start inquiries immediately.

Renee's care gave me time away from the stress. I had to push my fears to the back of my mind to give her the attention she needed and to achieve transfers that were becoming very hard for her. Eventually, all was done and logged.

I hurried back to Hyacinth's flat.

"I should not have brought Constance here. It is so easy to slip up on Covid regulations," I apologised.

"Where else could you bring her? Did Tanya say she was planning to stay over with a friend or anything?"

"No, she just left as soon as I got in. She hasn't seemed well for a couple of days and seems to be doing irrational things." I told Hyacinth about the hidden key and how it had been moved to a more obvious place as if she had been home and left suddenly.

"Did you hear her come in during the evening?" Hyacinth asked.

"I'm sure I heard the door click," I said, "but that was before I fell asleep."

Hyacinth looked at me sternly.

"I thought she had come home," I said defensively.

"Was she worried about anything?"

"There was the disappointment about the jobs and a bit of resentment about childcare for Constance, but nothing that seemed too much of a problem. She just looked a bit flushed and eager for some fresh air."

"Are you able to trace back her steps?"

"I will start at the sea front. Hortense dropped some hints about seeing lights from her window."

"Yes, go and look," agreed my mother-in-law, "but keep a check on the hours since you saw her and put in a missing person report if you don't find her soon."

I shuddered, cold, though the day was hot. I would have to cry off work too. I shrugged out of my uniform on the way back to the car and texted a message about a personal emergency to my employer.

I drew up in the car park and carefully aligned my search with the span of Hortense's view.

The promenade was a raised walkway above the level of the sands that fell away to a flight of steps nearest the town and rose to follow the line of the cliffs as it led further away. I decided to keep to the path to give me as wide a view as possible. I walked and tugged joylessly at Constance's hand until her pleas for a rest moved my conscience and I stood still, scanning back the way I had come and seeing nothing but the flat steely grey sea. The sands seemed empty except for a few boulders. I went slowly on, losing heart, but hoping to look back from a higher point to see the curving sweep back to the town.

"Look. Mummy, behind that rock. Can you see a thing like a bit of boat?" Constance pointed.

My eyes were not as good as hers, and I squinted as the sun broke the clouds, but I wanted to believe her. I needed a sign that Tanya was somewhere near.

A downhill, rapid walk led us back to the town's seafront and down the steps to the sand. The crisp, crumbling surface above the waterline slowed our footsteps. Once we walked further down onto wet sand, we could see the bow of a small boat wedged into the space between the wall of the promenade and the boulder.

"We almost couldn't see it, could we, Mummy?" Constance's was the joyous victory of a child who had no idea of harm.

I said, "Stay here; I will take a closer look."

She screwed her face and hung back, but still followed me.

Controlling myself firmly, I walked up the cloyingly soft, grainy beach to the half-hidden boat. There, cradled w-shaped over the oarsman's seat, was my daughter, covered in a fleece blanket that was stiff from the salt of the sea.

"Tanya!" my relief shouted as Constance clambered in beside her and gave her a warm hug.

Tanya opened her eyes slowly and pressed her hand to her head. Her cheeks were flushed, and she felt fevered as I touched her. I extricated Constance carefully from the boat as my fingers found 111 on the phone. Words tumbled from my mouth in response to the prompts about emergency services, location, and Tanya's condition. They said they would stay on the line, and I was to report any changes.

"How did you get here?" I asked.

"I came to see if the owner of the boat was here, but he wasn't back yet. It was right down there on the waterline. Tanya indicated vaguely in the direction of the sea. I was going towards it, and I felt faint. Did you pull it up and put me in it?"

I was alarmed. My mind recoiled from the enormity of the gap in our experiences overnight. "The paramedics will be here soon. They will check you over," I said to reassure both of us.

I wondered if she had hallucinated or if she had dreamed something and muddled it with reality.

The boat was firmly real under my hand, but there was nobody in sight and no footprints in the sand around it.

Puzzlement turned to practicality as other people began to gather on the beach. The first group to arrive were not the paramedics, though. It was the police, both uniformed and plain-clothed, siren-screaming their way to the edge of the promenade, leaping down to the sand, and waving on passers-by who had gathered to see some excitement. They had an incident tent which they proceeded to pitch over the boat, straddling it from one side to the other behind the boulder.

A female officer was asking Tanya to identify herself and give her age and address. A young constable tried to distract Constance, using his flat police cap to collect small, coloured pebbles from the beach around us. A female police officer stood beside me and edged me further from the boat.

I felt dumb, my motherhood invalidated. I blamed myself, my overpowering sleep last night, my commitment to a job that paid too little, my overconfidence that we would not catch Covid. I needed to be alone with my inadequacies or to share them with Hyacinth, or even Hortense, or to bury myself in giving perfect care to Renee.

"Miss Roberts," one of the officers was addressing me. She verified my name and address, confirmed that Tanya lived with me, and asked where I had last seen her and what had passed between us.

An ambulance's blue flashing light cut through the tears that hovered in my eyes; its green uniformed crew parked hefty equipment between me and Tanya's boat with electrodes, tubes, and gadgets to test her vital signs and calculate her oxygen. The police officers wove between them, taking measurements and samples, pushing the fleece blanket into a zip-lock plastic bag, and then stepping back for the medics to angle and lift my daughter onto their stretcher.

"I'm her next of kin," I expressed desperately to the officer who had been interviewing me.

"Yes, we know," she said. "She is conscious and has capacity so she can answer for herself."

"I am her mother," I said.

"We know, but she's an adult. She will answer for herself," insisted the police officer.

Tanya was wrapped tight as a mummy in a cellular blanket, with safety straps encircling the stretcher, making jerky progress up the beach, carried between two of the paramedics. The rest of the group followed with their equipment.

"Can I go in the ambulance with her?" I asked.

"You need to come with us to answer further questions at the police station," I was told.

The officer who had questioned me swept Constance up in her arms to carry her over the sand, and I heard her say, "Put me down, I want to walk with Mummy," before they went out of earshot.

Chapter Six
The Police Station

When I got there, my head protectively held as I left the car, I no longer heard Constance's voice. I looked around frantically on the short walk up the back steps into the interview room.

"I don't need to be here; I need to be with my daughter," I said.

The police officer was a different one. "Did you have any breakfast this morning?" she asked.

I looked at her, stunned as if that was important at this time.

"I'll send for some coffee," she said. They put two digestive biscuits beside the cup.

"Where is Constance?" I asked.

"She's safe. The social worker in charge of her case will come and introduce herself in a minute."

"What case?" I asked. "We've done nothing wrong."

"You are a single mother. Is there a father anywhere around?"

"He doesn't visit us. I raise her alone."

"That's what we thought. The social worker will be here shortly."

I thought of Constance swallowing weak orange squash and nibbling on a dry biscuit.

"She usually has cereal," I said.

"It's nearly midday now, Miss Roberts," as if it were proof of my neglect.

The social worker was cool and efficient. She asked me about my working hours and what my childcare arrangements were. She made a dissatisfied murmur when I said Tanya was my mainstay for Constance. She asked why Constance was not in school, and when I mentioned Covid, she said I was an essential worker, and there was a place in school for my child.

I wondered why she could not compute the difference between my hours and the average school day or why she did not realise a mid-morning or mid-afternoon break with my child was worth holding onto for as long as I could.

I was glad I didn't make my case aloud, though because now the police officers were back in the room. They were putting a camcorder on the table between us and were reading my rights into it as if I had conducted a felony. They asked if I had a lawyer and if I wanted one. I asked to phone Hyacinth.

"Hyacinth," I said. "Tanya is safe. They've taken her to the hospital. I am at the police station. They ask if I have a lawyer."

Panic was throttling me.

"Constance?" she was saying.

"With a social worker," I replied.

"I'll send you someone." Hyacinth put down the phone.

"They're on their way," I grunted to the police. I got a cup of tea this time. The camera was turned off while I had it.

After a while, an older man with a scrawny white beard sat beside me. I recognised him as the one who had written up the power of attorney I held for Hyacinth.

"It's like one hand washing the other," I muttered.

"What?" said the police officer, setting up back the camcorder.

"She said nothing," the lawyer said sharply, and I relaxed a little, feeling he would not let much past him.

The old familiar tale of Darfield's arrival and sudden departure from my life was trotted out.

In my defence, much was said about me being a homeowner with steady employment. Hyacinth was mentioned as my next of kin, and questions began about Tanya's role in my life.

"She's my daughter. She was still in her teens when we came to live here. She did FE and reached university entrance level."

"So, why hasn't she entered?" asked the eagle-browed officer on the other side of the camcorder.

"Question out of order," snapped my lawyer. "Tanya Roberts is of age. It is not my client's job to overrule her."

"Question withdrawn." The officer agreed.

"May I know how she is?" I asked, not bothering to notice the assumption they had made over her surname.

"You can go to the hospital as soon as we get you out of here," Hyacinth's legal friend patted my hand.

They turned their attention to the boat. Did I know whose it was? Had I seen it before? Did I know how it got up the beach? Why was I looking for it that morning?

"We can question your younger daughter in the presence of her caseworker," Eagle brows said as if to frighten me into revealing secrets they were sure I had.

I had no more knowledge of that boat than they had, but I told them how Hortense had watched it for two days and how she had said a platform was waiting out to sea for it.

This seemed to satisfy them, so they concluded the interview by logging the time into the camcorder.

"Can I get my child and go home?" I asked.

"The social worker will come and do an assessment," they promised.

"When?" I said, and my lawyer tapped me on the arm for silence.

"Come, I'll take you to the hospital," he said.

Chapter Seven
The Hospital

It was long after that I understood the compassion and the power of this little old man. Without telling me that I was, technically, still in custody, he negotiated the first step in my daughter's healing and turned me towards the restoration of my family life.

I stood silently, later that day, clothed in PPE, masked, and distanced from my child. I prayed silently for my companion. I begged earnestly for her life and realised that all the constraints that had shaped my adulthood so far had to fall away. No longer was I able to guide and protect her with my own strength. The fearful wrenching of a third birthing tore me open, giving me the first glimpse of a free spirit that might grow when mothering was over.

"You can take her hand," prompted the nurse who monitored Tanya's tubes and beeping screens. "We don't know if she can hear you, but we know they are sensitive to touch."

The 'they' pronoun that she used brought me to the consciousness of the rows of beds that held other people's relatives in ordered ranks along with this ward and in many others like them. I had been attending to my work, extending a time of unpaid childcare, getting on with my life as if Covid only existed for other people. I felt humbled, now, in my hospital gown, gloves, hat, and shoe coverings with my memories of the flimsy aprons, gloves, and masks of day-to-day caregivers.

The nurse brought my visit to a close to allow for 'procedures', she said. I was stripped of my visitor's accoutrements and shown my way back to the waiting lawyer.

"I don't recall your name," I apologised, wanting to acknowledge his vital and sudden role in my life.

"Bennett," he said, "but call me Paul."

"Okay, Paul. You accepted me as a mother when I most needed it. Thanks."

He seemed unable to catch my meaning and unwilling to be distracted by it. "We are returning for the second phase of your investigation now," he said, steering me away from the hospital grounds.

I stopped short, "But, Constance? The social worker said they were coming to my flat for an assessment. How can I not be there? They said she can't come home till they are satisfied."

"They won't go when you are not there," he reassured me as if I were a child.

I felt that Constance was being overlooked. Sharp agony pierced my voice, "But my child! I have two children!"

"Maybe, you should have thought of that before you became involved in this scenario," said Paul, unrelentingly leading me back to the interview room.

They popped up as if they had been waiting for me: the nameless brows who placed the camcorder and the female officer who prefaced the recording.

"The boat," she said. "Tell me about the boat."

"It was on the beach," I said.

"That was not the first time you saw it; take me over that bit again."

"It's the first time I recognised it. Constance pointed it out to me."

"Yes, your eyes are not good. Are they good enough to drive?"

"Question ruled irrelevant," muttered Paul.

"I accept that, Mr Bennett." Without turning her head, she said to eagle-brows, who lurked somewhere in the background. "Raise the eyesight report from the ophthalmologist and add driving to the charge sheet if you can."

I was weak in my shoes. They invalidated me as a mother; now, they attacked my ability to drive and, with that, went my livelihood.

"I have to provide for my children," I said.

"So, the boat enabled that?"

"The boat has nothing to do with me," I said.

"So, you were not involved in the transportation of refugees from Turkey who used your boat to cross the channel?"

I laughed out loud. "That little one-man rowboat!" There was an edge of hysteria to my voice. "Can that cross the Channel?"

"People are known to make it in blown up dinghies," was the rejoinder, ruled out by Paul's murmur.

"So, with such a sceptical attitude, you arranged for the platform. A holding place? A safe haven on the sea? An embarkation point just on the horizon, barely visible from the shore."

Alarm bells rang in my imagination. Where did they find all these improbabilities to string together?

"My daughter is ill in hospital with Covid," I tried to draw the conversation back to the only reality I could grasp. "I have no way of supporting my other daughter as long as you hold me here on trumped-up charges."

Paul hissed in my ear and patted my hand. I supposed he thought I should show no disrespect for their story structure.

"But, the boat, Miss Roberts. While your daughter was suffering from a high fever, what induced her to go to the beach alone at night in such mortal danger of collapse that your associate, whoever it was, had to make a bed in the boat and secure her until such time as you came to rescue her."

"I don't know what you mean. I don't have an associate or anyone except the Seaways residents and two daughters, who you have taken from me."

"Social Services has one, and the other is safely recovering in the hospital. The sooner you co-operate with our investigations, the sooner you will be able to go home and negotiate with the authorities to resume custody of Constance."

"Could you interview Hortense, please? She knows more about the boat and the platform than I do. She watches them day and night."

"Is this Hortense a person in your employ?" queried the policewoman.

"Hortense is my client."

"Hortense Coleman, Seaways resident." Paul and I spoke simultaneously.

The officer spoke into the camcorder. "Interview upheld for further inquiry." She switched it off. "Miss Roberts, it has been a long and tiring day. We will take you somewhere to sleep. A hot meal will be served to you shortly. Let the officer know of any dietary requirements."

Shortly, I lay as comfortless as Tanya. I prayed that Constance would have been feeling cared for safely that night. When exhaustion took over, I dreamed of a hospital bed alongside Tanya's where tubes entered and left our bodies, but still, our hands clenched us together, and hospital staff had to move around the far sides of our beds to attend to our needs.

Chapter Eight
Home

I don't know how Paul Bennett got me out, but I believe the bolt had slid back on my story when Hortense had entered it. They could not rush or force someone of her age and fragility, so investigations slowed down, and to hold me in a cell and feed me daily was beyond the police budget. I believe the magistrate referred to my status as 'release on bail' I surmised it was the time to tackle the Social Services and get Constance home.

She prattled as she came up the path, in true Constance fashion. "You see that window? I can climb in there if Mummy has gone out, and she hasn't left the key. She holds me on her shoulders, and I get ever so tall enough to reach the sill. You want me to show you?"

A man's voice replied, "Maybe, we won't need to. Maybe, she's here."

I couldn't hold back anymore. I was at the door, and she was in my arms, gloriously warm and comfortingly alive, dispelling fears of mortality and incarceration, chasing suspicion and unfounded accusations to their destination in unfocused memories.

I took her in, ignored the local government official, gave her cereal and lots of milk, and squeezed a fresh orange juice into her favourite cup.

He cleared his throat, "She's had breakfast at her foster home."

I turned my back to the kitchen table, leaned on it, and faced him, "I do not know of this foster home. I don't sanction it, and I will make whatever adjustments are necessary to get my daughter back. Now, I am making myself a cup of tea. You can have one if you want it."

He stumbled on his denial of needing anything. I pointedly ignored him and moved through the reassuring routine of providing for myself in my own kitchen.

"What problems do you have with me as a parent?" I sat bolt upright on a dining chair, haughtily angling my cup in his direction and gazing at him over the top of it.

"You work unsocial hours."

"All the better to have quality time with a school-age child."

"You rely on your elder daughter for unpaid, unqualified childcare."

"She is available to take a qualification. She neither works nor studies at the moment."

"Basic wage is nine pounds plus an hour."

"I know, I work for that myself. Hardly worth it if it's the total pay I get for my job, isn't it? And where's the tax to come from to pay the employer's share of it?"

"Exactly, so you can't afford to work," announced the social worker, getting up as if he had discharged his duty and Constance was to follow him out.

"She hasn't finished her cereal," I told him calmly," and you haven't started your environmental assessment.

He decided to relax. "Okay, I'll have that drink. Can you make it a coffee?" he asked.

While the kettle was on, I took him into Constance's side room with her evidence of toys heaped up, tablet frozen on the home-school page, and blue tacked pictures of Mummy and Tanya with legs and arms sprouting from their heads and 'I luv u' signs spidered beneath in preschool pencilled marks. I pointed to our two mezzanines above, which afford adult privacy to me, and Tanya, and he raised what he thought was a practised eyebrow querying the 'extra privacy required for visiting partners'.

"We don't have those," I snapped. "I am double-divorced and loving freedom, and Tanya is a young girl just out of FE with her whole life before her. Why would she want to clutter it up with men at this stage?"

He had the grace to look embarrassed but then sought to sting me back, "Yet there are irregularities about your home life. Constance has mentioned an absence of keys and dangerous incidents of her climbing through upstairs windows."

I had had enough. I reached for my phone and clicked, Paul. I told him the social worker was there in my space, hampering my access time with my child. He murmured in the way I had become used to. I clicked him off. A vibrating buzz began in the nameless social worker's pocket. He fished out the phone, held it to his ear, retreated to the garden, and remained here with a rapidly cooling coffee. Later, Paul called me back and said I was to have the night at home, but Constance would have to go back to her foster care to sleep, though, and she could stay with me until 6pm. I didn't care where Mr... I hesitated on his name to Paul, wishing I concentrated on words, not faces when people were introduced to me.

"Mr Phips," Paul supplied. "He will need to wait around within earshot, but next time you see Constance, she can come with her foster parent," he said.

I didn't care where he waited as long as it wasn't in my home. I savagely hoped it would rain and he would have to sit out in the dripping wet all day.

"How long will they take with Hortense?" I asked, eager to have the end of the police inquiries.

"How long is a piece of string?" Paul asked me.

So, the day passed balmily enough. I encouraged Constance to paint and draw, driving the topics ever more closely around our cliff walk, the long strides back to the beach, the sand, the boat, her sister's covered body, hoping that an angle or a spoken observation might make sudden sense to me, enable me, perhaps to unravel the suppositions that the police had formed about me and the boat.

Of course, I did not think of the human agency until Constance tired of artwork and went off to play with dolls in her room. Then, I heard her over and over again, saying, "Now, this is the boat, and I am going to tuck you safe in with this blanket because you've got Covid."

Hortense had seen the boat coming in. Boats don't usually drift onto our beach without human propulsion. The boat was built for one rower. Here was the person. If Hortense was right about the platform out at sea, that is where he or she came from and not without luggage, for where did the rower get the blanket from?

I realised I had a number for the coast guard somewhere. The phone rang, wanted verification of the number I had dialled, played a Covid warning, required a listed extension number, and was finally routed to a receptionist who wanted to know where the endangered vessel was. I described the seafront and said it was directly on the horizon opposite. I refrained from saying it was a platform. I wanted feedback. They gave me a website and an incident number as my username. I was grateful, sceptical, caught up with Constance, and anxious about the hovering presence of Mr Phips. I decided to offer him a sandwich just in order to check his exact whereabouts.

"I'm just going out to the garden a minute," I said through Constance's door from where I saw a range of boxes, prams, and buggies, each with a single doll covered by a scrap of cloth or a piece of clothes when the blankets had run out.

"Uhumm," she said, far too absorbed to bother.

I found the social worker a few feet from the gate, looking towards the rounded downs as if he really longed to go for a walk and take a look.

"You can leave us if you want to," I encouraged.

"No," he said, "you are not authorised to be alone with your child."

"Why, do you think I might take her and sell her to some random boat rower and bring your career down?" I was reckless of his goodwill, only capable of delivering withering scorn, not the offer of a sandwich that I had resolved to make. He did quail but gathered himself, turned towards me, past me, and took a seat on one of my garden chairs, right by my door.

I sniffed in disgust, swept by as if breaking a cobweb, and returned to Constance. She was walking a long-legged rag doll from imaginary boat to imaginary boat, then squatting him behind her bed watchfully.

"The rower," I said to myself. If he came from the platform with a blanket in his luggage, he needed his boat to get back, but by the time Tanya stirred, I had shown up, and then the seafront was crawling with police and paramedics, so where would the stranded rower have been? Was Constance right? Had he been just the other side of a boulder, watching us all along?

These questions demanded the attention of a quieter time. Meanwhile, I had a captive social worker here from whom I could prise cautions and warnings to protect my future parenting rights.

I made the sandwiches without asking now, a selection in case he was meat-free, dairy-free, or vegan.

No, he was gluten-free.

I wrapped the sandwiches in foil and stuck them in the fridge.

I found a pack of oat crackers and shoved them in his hand with another cup of coffee.

"So, if I give up my job, what benefits will I be able to claim?" I sat down with him to question.

They never give you straight information. "Do you rent this place?" he asked.

"It's on a mortgage," I said, a hint of pride in my voice.

He was crest-fallen, "You can't get rent rebates then or Council tax relief. Can you sell it?"

"And live where?" I asked.

74

"Social services can recommend you to a housing association in such circumstances," he regained confidence. "If you are technically homeless, we can rehouse you in a temporary shelter whilst you wait. I can ensure that the accommodation is child friendly so you can keep Constance with you."

The strategy of playing the plaintive worker, I thought. He was kinder when he felt in control.

"How would I cover living expenses even though they were reduced?" I asked.

Unemployment benefits, tax credits, a universal living wage, top-ups such as free school meals: all rolled off his tongue like a wound-up talking toy grinding out its pre-set messages.

I thanked him politely, picked up his empty cup, and leaned on the table to write the remembered list into the notebook I used for internet searches.

Constance was still busy with the leggy doll that was now sitting on a piece of scrap paper with a ruler balanced oar-like across its arms.

I went back to my informant. "And if I decided to start a business, what start-up grant could I attract?"

Now he was less certain, stumbling through vaguely recalled website names and stressing that loans were more common than grants and co-lateral was needed.

"So, to have an independent income, I need an independent home?" I demanded verification. "In my independent home, do I need to supply a more middle-class lifestyle for my child in order to qualify as a parent than the one I would need to offer on universal credit?" I demanded.

"Working parents are normally middle class, whilst benefitted families would be expected to supply their own childcare," he stumbled. Then his innate viciousness rose to protect him again. "You seem to want the best of both worlds: the right to work and the right to raise your own child."

I couldn't bother with this blithering mass of uncritical social assumptions any more. So, I was released to a happier tier of thought when Constance came out into the garden with the painted seascape held above her head. The leggy doll, its legs folded onto a square of paper, was held firmly to the painted waves by the other hand. The whole assemblage flapped softly in the afternoon breeze as Constance carried it triumphantly down the path.

"See, Mummy, he's going back out to sea now in his boat," she whooshed like a passing wave.

"Yes, and where is the doll he was looking after in it?" I asked.

"Gone to the hospital," she called back from the gate.

Chapter Nine
The Unknown

The afternoon was hazy and lazy. My unwelcome guest pushed out the odd comment intended as a conversation starter and I ignored it. Constance fitfully developed her scenario of the boy in the boat. I built a sea wall of containment around myself by bringing paints to the doorstep and developing an imaginary seascape with everything in it that figured in the investigation except the boy.

"You're very artistic," tried the social worker.

"We all are," I concurred without offering to explain who 'we' were.

Sarcastically, I thought of the police officers weaving their web of supposition, of Hortense connecting the flickering lights and shadows of the heavy sea into objects of solidity and purpose, of the government preaching on the daily news about following the science when science itself was just a string of propositions and rebuttals on the changing seas of coincidentally funded, tightly prescribed projects.

I deliberately cooked nothing. I fasted and gloried in my perfectly uninvaded body, suspended in its contemplation of the unknown. The occasional gurgle of Mr Phips's tummy filled me with triumph. If this were the only vengeance I could get for this unwanted intrusion in my life, I would relish it to the last grain of sand on the beach. I plied Constance with as much fruit, microwaved fish fingers, and chips as I could, even inventing a fishing net to dangle under her boat with crisp warm fishy morsels.

"Children need vitamins." was another try from Phips.

"Go over to the left. Towards the fence," I guided Constance. "You will find some tomatoes in a grow-bag there. Only pick the red ones. You will find them nice and sweet."

From under my eyelashes, I watched the social worker simmer down into a semblance of surrender to my absolute disregard. I gleefully visualised his backlog of casework growing higher with each forced hour of his precious wasted day.

I picked patiently and diligently over the events that led to the suspension of family life in my home.

Assuming that Constance was right and that a leggy boy was loitering on the beach, he would have been easily concealed by the rising side of the promenade as we walked up the cliff. Whilst our back was turned, he might have slipped out near to the town. I imaged his departing back as he loped towards the steps. It shimmered away in the glancing light of yesterday morning, as I reminded myself of Constance's insistence that she had glimpsed him high up on dry sand.

If he had hidden behind a boulder just a little further up from the half-concealed boat, could he have snaffled past the massed paramedics and advancing police cordon? Gauging time backward was a curious task, I found, realising that moments elongate in times of great concentration and shrink in the effort of action. Our walk up the hill must have occupied us for at least half an hour, our stride down maybe for ten minutes. The moment when I found Tanya in the boat behind the rock followed another ten minutes as we wove our way a much shorter distance across the sand and between the boulders. My shocked call for help, effected within five minutes, was followed by an indeterminate wait for medical help, and an eon of police interference.

A quick snort of slumber resistance escaped the social worker. One conscious eye blinked at me and then closed again, as if his interest in my case were stifled by its inactivity.

I exchanged my paints for a pencil and a linen board for paper. I drew an architectural bird's eye view of the beach, its boulders, the raised promenade, flotsam, and the boat. I drew sightlines from each to each and past each. I tried to figure out where the boy must have been from moment to moment during the walk we took up to the cliff, then back down to the sea. At what stage he had covered my daughter and whether he had cradled her, or she had entered the boat and collapsed there, I may never know but I grew certain that he had been there, watching and caring, until he was sure she had been found.

Whether he knew I was her mother, I queried. He may well have been in earshot of Constance's cry, "We almost couldn't see it, could we, Mummy?" but would he know I was mother to both of them?

I called Tanya's name, but she did not reply when she woke up. The difference in age between my children did not indicate that they were siblings. Even now, in the town, many people assume that Tanya was a young mother, and I was Constance's grandmother.

So, the boy almost certainly knew she had been found, but possibly nothing more.

Was he waiting on the beach to get back his boat? Assuming it was his boat, did he think that she would be found and taken away for care, clearing the way for him to row back to sea to the platform if it really existed? He had calculated without the thoroughness of the British Police.

I, though, was sitting here, dismissing the evidence my daughter just gave me. He would have been waiting for his boat back. Having it, he could have headed back to some larger vessel from which he came. When officialdom destroyed his plan, where did he go?

I visualised the unknown boy, stranded on the beach, with no means of returning to sustenance, shelter, and company, cooped in away from the steps and the town by a busy police investigation that sought, yes, I had to face it, to implicate and to criminalise me.

My outrage drew a cry to my lips which I quickly stifled when I saw the one eye flicker in my direction again. This time, it did not close, the wrist came up, and the eye, joined by the other one, focused on the timepiece.

"It's five o'clock, Miss Roberts; don't you think you should put together some clothes for Constance to take back to her foster home?"

I swallowed hard, "And toys. She'll need her things," I strangled.

"No toys. She will find plenty there. This is Covid time. We don't want unnecessary sources of infection, do we?"

"Toiletries?" I was panicking for time.

"Only packaged and unused. A toothbrush and toothpaste will be fine."

80

"Oh!" I was made immovable by the pulsating finality of it all.

"Well, go on, then," he prompted with the hint of a kind smile. "Time is going; we leave here at five forty-five."

"You said, six o'clock," I accused him of robbing my time with Constance.

"Six o'clock is my logging out time. I have to have her safely installed by then."

Confused about the increased pace of adult activity that followed, Constance abandoned the seascape and its flimsy cardboard and cuddled the leggy doll on the doorstep.

Mr Phips, grasping a pink backpack decorated with cartoon mermaids, bent to raise her from there all too soon. I stretched my arms to hug my daughter; Mr Phips told her to give me the doll. She resisted. He marched her down to the garden gate. Speeding after them, I nearly tripped on the doll that he flung back over.

I heard his parting shot, "Mummy will look after that for you." The car door slammed. Her muffled cries were overpowered by his engine firing and revving away.

My tears burst their banks. I clicked Paul's number to protest.

"The police are on their way for you. They are ready for the next phase of the investigation. Put a bag of toiletries together," he said, ignoring my outpouring.

I screamed into the flannel, bit the toothbrush to silence myself, stuck bits and pieces into a supermarket paper carrier, and combed my hair, long and smooth like a mermaid, to calm myself and appear elegant and controlled before my interrogators. On an impulse. I reached for a uniform. Professional attire gave a persona of outward efficiency. I

81

would wear it. No, that one needed ironing. I grabbed the one I wore the day before and stuffed it into the top of the paper bag.

I methodically closed and locked all the windows. Checked the utilities were switched off. Double locked the door and pocketed the key. I went to lean on the gate and await the police, the leggy doll clutched to my chest.

Chapter Ten
The Boy

He represents the boy, I told myself, over and over again, as I stared at the doll, dry-eyed, in the back of the car. I was using that short drive to penetrate what I knew of this unknown stranger and what Constance had been trying to show me.

Children have their own intuitive style of thought, though, we may reason to create stories; they associate and see links that we miss. If Constance was clear that the boy needed his boat to get back out to sea, she would expect that he remained on the beach. This being the case, where was he now?

Since he didn't go out to sea or turn towards the town, he must have climbed around the boulder-strewn shore to the base of the cliffs where they tumbled past the retaining wall of the promenade.

At some stage, the sea defences must give way to untrammelled steepness above, which was the smoothness of the downs.

I wished I had been more curious about the coast beyond the promenade, but such adventures were limited with a preschool child and a full-time job.

They were capping my head again to guide me out of the car. The interview room was ready, equipped with a steaming cup of coffee and a sandwich of some kind of yellow stuff. Paul was seated neatly to the right of the empty chair, and a male officer was preparing to switch on the camcorder.

"Where's the policewoman who was questioning me before?" I asked Paul, catching the man's mouth as it began to form his words and leaving it soundlessly open.

Paul cleared his throat and looked apologetically at the officer.

"She's off duty," he said.

"I want to be interviewed by a female," I said.

"There are no suggestions of sexual misconduct," Paul said irrelevantly.

"I did not say there were, but I am a mother, being queried about my care of my child."

Paul's eyebrows raised at the construction I put on the proceedings. "Fair enough, it will cause a delay," he said, "but it is your right to request if you are certain you have the time to spare."

"My time is not my own just now," I acknowledged, watching balefully as the camcorder was switched off and the male officer excused himself to the uniformed attendant who stood against the wall behind me.

I swallowed the coffee and nibbled one edge of the bread, pushing the plate as far from me as possible instead of tasting its yellow innards.

"Haven't you eaten today?" asked Paul as if to fill the gap made by the police reshuffle.

"I fasted all day," I snapped.

"Oh," he seemed taken aback by the religious terminology, "Perhaps a cup of soup then?"

"I continue fasting," I fixed him with a priestess-like stare, and he shrunk silent as if before a superior power.

Yes, my authority was strong and long-lasting, I thought, gratefully, as I counted the years that separated my two children and added on months of visible pregnancy and years of pre-schooling motherhood to reach this day when all was being called into question. By what? A boy.

I took the doll from my lap and arranged him cross-legged and squared on loppy arms across his knees. I slid him, totem-like, across the desk, halfway to the interrogators' seat and able, if alive, to turn his head to each of us alternately. As it was, he stared steadily and blankly at Paul.

This is it, I thought. He represents my hope of freedom, Tanya's hold on life, and my custody of Constance.

I settled down in thought about the issue of where that boy went when the rest of us left the beach.

I re-wandered up the promenade to the clifftop. Somewhere from there, I could locate the cemetery that stood on a lower rise on the other side of the rounded hill. To the right the headland would fall away from the tumbled rocks to the shore. The boy may have skirted them on his way over the rounded head, then down to the cemetery. In my imagination, he saw an advancing tide, realised he could not turn back to the town beach, and set himself to clamber and slide his way up the rocky side to the head of the cliff.

He tested the higher rocks with his fingers and dug in his toes with each perilous step. My eyes were fastened on the doll with lengthy and flexible legs and arms that gave him the reach he needed if his hands and footholds were far away from each other.

I saw them bring back the camcorder but paid no attention till they fixed it and announced the interview.

"So, who owns the boat?" the woman sergeant asked.

"The boy," I said, refusing to look up at her.

"Which boy?"

"Him," I said, pointing at the doll.

"Miss Roberts, are you light-headed? You haven't eaten, have you?"

"Immaterial," said Paul. "Miss Roberts claims a religious right to her practices."

I nearly choked. Was he suggesting a fanatic? It was summer, not Lent. Was it Ramadan?

"A boy," questioned the sergeant. Did she say she was a sergeant? She wore a bright red dress and jacket.

You need pearls on that neckline, I thought irrelevantly, it contrasts too much with the pallor of your skin. Aloud I said, "The boy was exactly like him, long, lanky arms and legs and no flesh. Very slim. Very lithe," I desperately wanted to validate my image of him climbing free of the incoming tide up the next scarp to our town's gentle seafront.

"The colour of his skin?" she prompted.

"I don't know, tanned, darker than you."

"Clean-shaven or stubbled?" she asked.

"Just a boy," I insisted, "soft, downy growth, no beard yet."

"Hair?"

"Longish, windswept, wet. It had rained in the night," I insisted.

"If it had rained, why was the blanket dry? It was stiff with seawater, but it was not wet when we bagged it."

She was sharp, this lady. I started to feel respect, one professional to the other.

"If it was dry, he'd used a tarpaulin," I pointed out, reviewing the police activity whilst, according to my summation, he was hiding behind a nearby boulder.

My imagined picture of him climbing the rocks was revised to show a twisted, tucked, plastic tarpaulin secured around his neck as he scrambled methodically upwards.

"His neck was long," I added to my description.

"Does he match this photofit?" questioned the sergeant, reaching for a tablet from the officer who stood behind me.

"More or less," I said, checking with Constance's assertions, her choice of toy, and my reasoned imaginings. "My eyesight is not wonderful."

"We know, Miss Roberts. We have that on our charge sheet."

She was strangely unthreatening. She stood up.

"Is that all you need to know?" I asked.

"I am going to follow up your lead with this young man," she said. "My colleague wants to know more about the boat. Are you sure you won't have that sandwich?"

I looked at the dry, curling edges, and my lip involuntarily curled to match it.

"No?" She was non-judgemental and considerate. "Something hot?"

"All day breakfast," I said, ironically.

"Fine," her eyes twinkled, and she slid out past the man who had been waiting for my guard to drop and who now lowered himself heftily into the interviewer's seat.

"It's getting late," he said.

"Sorry, but I guess this is your night duty," I manoeuvred into control as he admitted human weakness.

He sighed, mussed his hair, and told the camcorder that he was Inspector Parks.

"The boat is registered to a foreign port. Why is this?" he said.

"I suppose because the boy is a foreigner," I replied.

"But you have been using this boat to bring in asylum seekers from overseas," he stated.

"Who have I brought in?" I asked.

"It is we who ask the questions and you who answer," he warned. "Let's try again," "Where do you put boys like this one?"

"I have no boys to put," I patterned his language as if it was limited.

"Then, why did your daughter go down to the beach to meet this boy?" he asked.

So that was it. They thought she had an assignation, maybe an attachment.

"She didn't go to meet anyone. She went for a walk because she was flushed and needed some air."

"On a rainy night?" he pressed.

"It wasn't raining yet."

"And was she in the habit of going for walks when you came home from work?"

"No, but the pandemic has stymied her chances of employment, and she is expressing frustration about being so often left to care for her younger sister."

"Okay, so we have sorted out the child-care issue for you. Do you think she will still be needing night walks to the beach?" Paul rumbled beside me. The officer changed his tack.

"If the boat belonged to the boy, why was your daughter in it?"

"I was not there. At the end of a night when she didn't come home, I was grateful to find her safe anywhere."

"Why didn't you notify the police that she was a missing person?"

My mind travelled back to that night of delayed, paralysing slumber preceding the next day's early start.

"Sometimes the interval between the night calls and the next mornings are so brief that sleep is the only demand your body can respond to," I said.

My red-dressed woman squeezed through the door behind him and slid a covered food box in front of me, followed by a takeaway cup of orange juice.

"Besides, I expected her back before morning," I finished, with a sense of relief, "and we found her, me, and Constance, sheltered carefully by the boy. Now he is your problem, not me."

I firmly opened the box and started to eat. He had no option but to turn off the camcorder unless he wanted a record of my chewing sausage and bacon and slurping orange juice from an over-filled cup.

Chapter Eleven
The Boat

I snooze after eating at the best of times. This was not the best of times, so I sank into my torpor, regretting the slowing I associated and resisted with age but hazily eager for the respite it offered.

The boy had climbed up the cliff with the tarpaulin wrapped around his neck. He had looked down inland to the cemetery and had strolled between gorse and heather to its perimeter on the far side of the drive-in entry, where the road petered out and became a trodden path up through the trees.

He had just turned left, the woven tarpaulin catching on low-hanging branches as he passed when they rapped on the table and woke me up.

"What time is it?" I asked, the involuntary waking thought of all front liners when they break between one shift and the next.

"Not for you to worry about," blanked the male inspector while Paul gently permitted, "Nine-twenty pm."

"Your wife will want you home in forty minutes," I said to Officer Parks, his name jumping into my mind. "I thought it was later than this. I thought this was your night duty."

"It could turn out to be a double shift." He said it as if he was prepared to negotiate, mollified by my uncharacteristic attention to his name.

"Oh, I just remembered because the last thing in my awareness was of the police cars parking at the steps."

"Your awareness?" he queried as Paul stiffened.

"Before my life as a mother caved in by the certainty that my eldest could have died of Covid and the swift removal of my youngest to foster care," I amplified.

"Ok, so the boat is a necessary part of trafficking."

Paul harrumphed loudly.

"How much does it make per trip?"

"I don't know."

"Do you collect the money?"

"If I did, why would I work?"

He ignored the protocol of me not questioning him in order to make his own assumption. "You need a cover, just like any other nefarious operator. There is no rationale in working so hard, driving at your own expense to barely cover the car costs, doing without the advantages of status for children you obviously care about. Your mortgage is very small. You paid a huge proportion for a desirable flat, six or seven years ago. Do you think we don't watch those who take up residence in our town?"

Paul's rumble became a growl, and Parks subsided.

I lengthened his silence to his full discomfort by slowly sipping from the orange juice. He tried a new tack.

"You received signals on the seafront two nights ago. You flashed back answers. This was the very night the boat came in."

My look of astonishment met his eyes over the empty juice cup.

He pressed his advantage, "We have evidence from two separate residents of Seaways. One is prepared to testify in court against you."

I thought of Hortense, her aquiline nose twitching with excitement as she inserted television-quality narrative into her sightings of lights and shadows from her window. Yet, the realism of her accusation brought me up short when I took account of the boat. Its rough wood was overlaid by hard, thick paint. The measured spaces from stem to bow between which my daughter was lodged, the narrow space above and around it, quickly clothed by the police incident tent, the careful, rolling, cradling care of the paramedics once their preliminaries were done, "Will she live?" I asked, filled with dread that my life will never resume.

"Oh, yes," Officer Parks replied. "Your client is made from strong stuff. We examined the remnants of the food and drink you gave her. Had you intended to contaminate them in any way, you had not succeeded this time. He shut up as Paul made to stand. Subsiding to silence, I thought, cheekily undermining a parallel professional. Who was going to look after him when he got old if this was his opinion of health care workers?"

"You are a boat owner," he emerged from the snub undaunted, "but you don't operate your boat. You leave that to illegal immigrants who work between this shore and a raft out to sea."

I wondered how long he had sat in Hortense's room being regaled by her story spinning.

Paul cleared his throat and warned Officer Parks to substantiate his allegations about the ownership of the boat before he pressed this aspect of the case any further.

I listened wide-eyed as the analysis was delivered of the value of my London flat, the sale value of goods I did not bring down to the coast. The size of my mortgage and the amount of money I retained, presumably for 'nefarious' purposes. This, he compared with the purchase price of the boat and said its paperwork was linked with my name in London before I registered it in France.

The perfection of the story took my breath away. "You should write for TV," I said.

He looked flattered.

"But how?" I asked. "Did you not check the veracity of the ownership documents? Didn't you know about internet fraud and loss of identity? Forged signatures? I know about it, and I am just a health care worker. I have to check my bank account. I have had to dial an emergency number as figures slipped from my balance. I have to shred arbitrary piles of personal correspondence and separate the cuttings into successive waste collections to maintain the integrity of my accounts. I deny the ownership of this boat, and the burden of proof is on you."

They released me from custody that night. I travelled home in Paul's car, arriving after midnight and falling asleep on the settee, surrounded by Constance's dolls and wrapped in her blankets and dressing gown. Dawn found me awake and energised, walking down the town, onto the seafront, and along the base of the promenade to the boulder that had hidden the boat. The police paraphernalia had all gone. The boat had gone; the dry sand was raked smooth where it had lain. Was there no court case hanging over my head? I would conclude it was all a bad dream in response to the loss of my children, one to Covid and one to care.

Well, they weren't dead. I told myself, rising to the full lioness mode of motherhood. I would get them back. The battle had just begun.

Chapter Twelve
The Raft

The raft is a survival mechanism, I told myself. My survival is to know my children are well. That boy needed his boat to reach the raft. I needed my children to feel alive.

I phoned the hospital. Tanya was out of danger. I phoned Social Services. They uhum-ed and ahh-ed about visiting rights. I phoned Paul and caught him in bed, having had a sleep-in. I argued a tight case and demanded access with Constance the same day, reiterating Mr Phips's assertion that her foster parents would bring her to see me. He said he would do his best and called back to say he had a magistrate's hearing in two days' time. Well, it was a wait, but it needn't seem a long one.

The raft was still out at sea.

I tidied the house, hung all the clothes, folded all the blankets, arranged the dolls on the tops of cupboards, looking down proudly at the restored order. I packed lunch, a flask, a pair of binoculars, and a plastic mac into a shoulder bag, took a long, hooked stick that I kept in the garden, and left the house. My phone was in my pocket. My head was high, and I was going raft hunting.

It was a long walk to the top of the cliff. I hadn't realised the distance when I hauled Constance part way up. Then I had left the car in the seafront car park; now, I had walked from my flat because I was tired of people watching my movements and interpreting them in a way that suited their own private narrative. I, fleetingly, wished I had included dark glasses in my bag, but I figured out they might obscure my vision, and I couldn't use them at the same time as binoculars anyway. I lengthened my stride and relaxed my shoulders, settled in for a steady climb up a steepening and narrowing path.

When it narrowed out, I was near the top of the cliff's swell, and a brief dip full of brambles separated me from the top-most peak from which the open sea could be viewed. I used my stick to draw aside the treacherous spines and trails that crossed my path, set my foot against roots that sprouted up the hillside and scrambled through the bushes to the promontory. There, shielded from the curious gaze of dog walkers and serious ramblers, I spread my mac, sat on it, arranged my food and my flask, and expectantly raised the binoculars.

The focus was crazy. The range was limited. I saw nothing but kaleidoscopic blue waves winking in the sunlight. I had not come out for nothing, I told myself. The police believed in the raft. The boy came from the raft and, up till now, was probably wishing he could get back there. Hortense had spied the raft and was convinced she could link it to a story of my guilt. Officer Parks believed her and was looking forward to using her as the chief witness in my prosecution. I needed to believe it more than all of them. I would persist until I saw it.

As I waited for the light to change, I drank coffee, ate sandwiches, and nibbled half-ripe blackberries that hung on a few sun-facing branches. I learned to train the binoculars, line up the lenses into a single field of vision, and zoom in close to the waves by twirling the bit in the middle. How did I have these things? Magpie-like, I had brought them from London with other unused but useful remnants of my past. I could not remember now whether they were from Algie or Darfield. That was immaterial; what was important was to use them as a tool to get back their daughters.

In the later afternoon, and early evening, the sun slanted across the sea instead of hitting it at a ninety-degree angle of blinding brightness. Then, I started to distinguish between the distance and shape, knowing which objects move and mutated and which were static. I trained the twin lenses carefully back and forth along the horizon until I located two erect poles that seemed to sprout from the sea.

"Ahh," I spoke aloud, "here you are, now show me something more about you."

I turned the focus to sharpen it as much as I could. I fancied seeing head shapes pushed above the parapet between the poles. I waited for more, for the sun to lower and lights to come on. There was a rustling in the bushes below me. I shrank down, loathe to be seen, unwilling to inflame the allegations against me, hugging the vision of the raft to me as I should have been hugging my children. Just below my sight line, the rustling stopped, and I sat up cautiously, straining to see who stood below me on the cliff edge. I saw the top of a head, a long slim hand, fingers, boyish, and gnarled, grasping a white cloth which he waved in the breeze and whirled and waved for as long as his slim strength endured. Then the hand fell, and the head lowered with a scrunch, as if he had squatted down in his hollow to wait.

He waited and I watched. We were silent partners now, in the conundrum caused by borders and barriers. Countries and customs, custodies and citizenships, visas and visiting rights: they were all procedures to prevent the rights of relationship and the benefits of belonging. I respected his privacy, as I hoped he would mine, should our paths cross when leaving. Whyever, he needed to attract the folks on that platform and whether he would manage to re-join them, I was now secure in the knowledge that it was there, and that the boat's origin had nothing to do with my alleged ownership of it.

I looked at the binoculars hanging from my neck again. The string ended in a knot of tape, threaded through a small D ring, too narrow for the manufacturer's original cord to pass through. Whilst the boy waited, motionless, I started to carefully unpick the tape. One of my children's fathers had refastened the cord following some slight damage to a split ring like the one that remained on the other side. I soundlessly and persistently eased out its compressed scrawniness till it came loose, and the binoculars slid, plop, onto my mac.

The boy looked up. Then stood, startled as a young hare, and craned his delicate neck up to my lair. I stretched my fingers to him, almost for him to sniff, as I would to a half-wild creature I had startled. He drew back, almost toppled into the treacherous air that wafted across the headland. I stretched a hand purposefully to steady him then, and he grasped it, pulling just enough to manage the almost perpendicular climb that had not been a part of his plan. I patted the place beside me and passed him some food that he wolfed hungrily. Then I passed him the binoculars, and he trained them on the platform, waving his white flag joyfully.

I did not know if he knew who I was. I was convinced he was the boy from the beach, the one who had watched over Tanya, maybe the one who had kept her safe all night. I wondered if he had a tarpaulin somewhere.

He sat beside me, motionless on the mac, waiting. His eyes pierced the lowering light of the summer sun, occasionally raising the binoculars for another look. So as not to intrude, I silently smoothed and smoothed the ancient tape. How old? Seven years or twenty-one years? I interrogated it noiselessly, discovering it was one of those name tapes soldiers stitched into their uniforms. D., it answered, Darfield, not Roberts? I was disappointed. I didn't want any piece of him. It took away the sentimental value of the binoculars, relegating them once more to a marginally useful; now, I know, rather frustrating category of jumbled memories.

Yet, lights were winking out to sea, and the boy was jumping happily, pointing. "Darfied, Darfied!" He was saying. He thrust the binoculars back at me and plunged down the cliffs, then loped to the landward side as swift and sure as a goat.

I came to myself. There was a darkening sky. I was alone, way up the cliffside, with a phone that was losing its charge. I stuffed all the items I had brought with me back into the bag. I had my hook stick in my hand, and I traced the crashing sound of the boy's steps down the hillside between the two cliffs, using the stick both to steady myself and to push aside the clawing vegetation.

I emerged through a hedge when the boy's steps had become soundless. I found myself opposite the cemetery driveway, with the soft trodden path to my right. I was sure he had gone that way. I looked up and saw the low-hanging branches swaying more than the breeze warranted. I wasn't going after him, though. My objective had been to see the raft, and I had seen it. More so, its connection to the beach and the boat was proven by the boy's presence, his frantic signalling, and his evident conclusion that they had seen him when a light answered his waving. Tomorrow was another day to follow through with the coincidence of seeing him. I would return to this corner and follow the path up through the woods again.

Chapter Thirteen
Hortense

I had no more use for or interest in the binoculars. I pondered. They had never been a part of my life, unlike the paints Algie had left me, used, and lovingly replaced over the years as my skills with them grew. I was not bonded to them by good memories like the flasks of Tanya's baby days or the blankets Constance dangled inextricably from her fingers while she sucked her thumb. I had arbitrarily brought all small objects from my flat in London to this new home, only cashing in larger, valuable objects to pay for removal costs and legal fees. I always expected that I would sift through and throw out when I had time, but mothering had been my sole preoccupation. Now, I had the rest of that evening and part of the day tomorrow to make some inroads on the clutter. If I could find that boy at some stage, I would give him the binoculars.

I started in the easiest place, with the photos, which I balanced on my lap on the settee, eating Jamaican bun and cheese and drinking hot chocolate in tribute to Hyacinth and all the love she had given me.

I went through the layer of photographs that captured Constance. It was a thin one, modified by mobile phones and tablets. I sorted through agent-supplied photos of both flats: the one I had sold and the one in which I now lived. I came to the scatterings through my life of Darfield, where I took the army label from my pocket and placed it at the bottom of his pile as proof of his ownership of the object. I was about to give it away. His accusation was always that I was a thief. I had stolen the attention of his army buddy, stolen Tanya's chance of a normal family life, planned to steal back my right to an independent existence, and, once successful, had stolen his own daughter in a custody battle.

"Yes, Darfield, handsome and untrustworthy, I am nearly finished with you. Are you finished with me yet?" I said to his portrait picture as I laid it over his crumpled name tape.

I picked up and binned a number of snapshots of him with colleagues from civilian and army life, one or two pictures of family weddings, him standing head and shoulders over other relatives and some with Tanya when she was small and trusted him too much. I did not want to linger over the memory of him loosening her shoulder straps and touching her skin where breasts would come, so I ditched all holiday photos of that era. Some double portraits of him with older family members were there, taken, perhaps at weddings or significant anniversaries. I would save them for Constance as evidence of her forbears. I glanced at each with a little interest in tracing resemblances as I leafed through them. Eye shapes here, a turn of the mouth there, some still hidden in baby fat but maybe characteristics to come as she grew older.

My idling fingers stiffened suddenly. Here was Darfield, sitting at a table with a woman hovering behind his shoulder whose nose I knew. The aquiline shape, even the admonishing finger, hovering near it, was unmistakably Hortense! What was she doing among Darfield's aunts, uncles, and cousins? Surely this couldn't be the reason for her dismissive but exaggerated demands on my time whenever my duties led me to her flat.

I was confused, overwrought by the absence of my children and the predicament of my arrest, I told myself, trying to discount this new awareness.

I reached for the paper bag of the day, anxious to put on my uniform and go and confront her. I clicked the phone to assure my office that I was free to work that evening.

They said, "good," but my rota had been covered already. I did not need to work again till after the weekend.

I wondered if the next week's work was already on my phone. If it was, I would have Hortense's number. The coming days of work had not been transferred to my personal phone yet. I felt even more determined as I studied the photo in my hand and decided I would not wait to query my discovery undercover as a company carer. I was his daughter's mother. Constance was Darfield's child. If she was related to Hortense. I needed to know.

The mobile's charge was definitely low. I plugged it in and clicked on Hyacinth in the contact list. As it rang, I put it on the loudspeaker, so that it could remain safely plugged in.

Hyacinth's welcome was as warm as ever, asking about each of my children in turn and commiserating with me for Tanya's hospitalisation, whilst she rejoiced to hear that the worst was over, and Tanya would soon be out. She asked about Constance, and this was trickier to negotiate. I decided to say that she was with friends. She snapped silent for a minute, then seemed to overlook issue of Covid restrictions making a visit an unlikely. Indeed, our visits to her had been similarly outside of government guidance.

I managed then to raise my concern, pushing guilt aside as I used my mistake of leaving uncompleted notes to justify my request for contact with Hortense. My strategy worked. In a few minutes. Hyacinth telephoned Hortense. Hortense called me back, eager to know where I had been and why my work had been left unfinished.

I told her that there was Covid in the family, so I had to stay off until I had taken a test. This satisfied one query. "But Hyacinth said you had left a gap in my notes," she reported.

"Yes," I said. "It was one of those nights when we were caught up with lights from the boats and the platforms out at sea."

"Just one boat and one platform. Don't exaggerate, Miranda," she corrected.

"Yes, but I would have corrected it on my next visit if I'd not been off," I explained, wondering how I could work around this to the topic of Darfield.

The platform gave me the lead, aided by the binoculars. "I do believe you are right, by the way," I mentioned with a show of casual chatter. "I was out with Darfield's binoculars today, and I was able to see details of this platform that you are watching."

The change of tack worked. "Darfield's binoculars? I haven't seen him in ages, I am not sure I have even mentioned his name in your presence or that you have any connections with him in the belongings left from your ex-husband."

"I doubted it too," I admitted with genuine innocence. "But a label came loose from the binocular's strap today with an initial D."

"Well, I never!" exclaimed Hortense in artful curiosity. "Now, what may that have to do with me?"

"There was a photograph in my box showing you and Constance's father together," I stated nonchalantly. "It was thrown in amongst other snaps taken with various relatives."

"Indeed," murmured Hortense politely, "Do you think I'm his aunt?"

"That did occur to me," I said, heavily sarcastic and relieved that the question clarified their relationship with no further probing.

She withdrew like a scorpion ready to strike, "Miranda, I know you merely as a professional, one who attends me. I employ a company that happens to schedule you for many of my calls. If we share family members, either current or past, that can be considered a conflict of interest and should be reported to your employer."

"What about the presence of a platform that you insist I notice every time I do a call with you?" I was reckless with my career now. I could have lost my children because of her obsession. I began to suspect that she did know more of my past with Darfield than she admitted, and the single word repeated twice by my silent boy rang in my memory. "Darfied," he had said, "Darfied." It was simple to conclude that the effort of getting his tongue around a name that was foreign to him swallowed the 'l' that was so familiar to us.

"Confirm one thing," I requested with no pretence of civility. "Are you Darfield's aunt?"

"Yes," she said and slammed down the phone.

I smoothed the name tag in my hand again as if it were my nerves, I was steadying. I placed it squarely on the photograph of Darfield with Hortense and slid them onto a shelf under my clock.

At nine-twenty, I had a call from my supervisor at work. "Hi, Miranda, how are you?" She began with an inquiry about my health and my lack of symptoms. "Miranda, you offered to work this evening," she recalled. "I am glad we were able to endorse your time off until Monday. However, I shall need to see you on Monday morning before you return to work. I have had a disturbing report that you failed to complete the log in Hortense's flat the night before your isolation. This is a grave lapse of due diligence, and I need to suspend you until it has been thoroughly investigated."

"I did fill in the MAR chart, though, when I administered her drugs and that is more vital than the daily log," I spoke up in my defence.

"They are both legal documents," my superior stated the obvious. "Our company cannot condone lack of due diligence. I will send you the time of our meeting as soon as it can be fixed."

I flung down my phone repeating, "A small job is better than no job at all," and making it a chant to ward off the prospect of unemployment, a long-term consequence of lack of diligence. That almost became a part of the chant too, but I could not tolerate a total abysmal loss of self-esteem, so I consoled myself by packing a bag for tomorrow, a canvas one, this time, that would not disintegrate at the bottom as yesterday's bag threatened to do, particularly when I abstractedly turned to pick rejected and forgotten early blackberries out of its corners.

Chapter Fourteen
Hyacinth

It was too late to call back Hyacinth, even on the pretence of thanking her for prompting Hortense to call me. The exasperation of my company was significant if they had decided to respond to Hortense's complaint at nearly ten o'clock at night. It was too late to phone Paul to follow up or hasten his plan for my access with Constance, but I could check my messages to see if he had sent anything more. I felt like Tanya, needing air, and I wondered when the hospital would send her home. Discharge plans were always vague, wavering between doctors' availability to see patients and sign them off and ambulances' capacity to transport them. News now was that incoming patients had to wait in the emergency vehicles for spaces on the wards. What with the in-depth cleaning before they were required again, delays would be hampering every end of the system. I went upstairs to prepare Tanya's side of the mezzanine, making sure that each of the commitments of the coming day would slot in beside each other so that no one need be neglected, and each member of my small family would be aware of my lasting love and constant cherishing.

Tanya's room was full of dress jewellery tangled over stands and into boxes, college papers bursting out of folders, clean clothes tumbled onto chairs, and partly worn ones in colour-coded heaps on the floor. The bed was pulled back, but a fresh cover had been put on the duvet, so I pulled it up and sorted papers onto the bed.

I found a letter to Hyacinth.

"Dear Hyacinth," I read.

"Mummy says that because of Covid precautions I cannot visit you, but I really wanted your advice about my future. You see, when I stood out on the beach, cooped up against Mummy and Constance in that ridiculously small triangle that is the only bit you can see from your window, and when I received and refracted back the little bursts of light you sent from your room, I was amazed by a sense of failure and claustrophobia. I could not allow my life to be swallowed up by small jobs in a small town, or even to be delayed by any more irrelevant college courses. I want to breathe, Grandma. I want to live in the fresh air. I want the hills I walk down to be full of lush purple, red, and green fruits, like yours, were when you carried your basket on your head. What can I do, Grandma, what turn can I take? How can I prevent this time of lockdown from swallowing me up and forcing me into a smaller mould than the wax I'm made of should fill?"

The sentences stopped here, but lower down the page there was a desperate scrawl, "Grandma, help me." There was a date and time: July 20, 2020, 9.30pm.

This was just a few days ago, the day Tanya left here, just a few minutes before my return: that was the day she had gone back to the seafront and watched for lights… The same lights Hortense stared at daily…

A creeping fear prickled from under my skin. A confusing fear that asked if Darfield were still in her life. Was he trying to creep back now that she was an adult, to steal her from under my nose? Was he going to press his distorted claims of familiarity with her in order to corrupt the wholeness of our family? Did he need to satisfy his ego and feed his spite by destabilising the unity of my brood?

Was he using his aunt for this purpose? Did he send a boat to this particular piece of the shoreline because of us?

I couldn't call Hyacinth, but I could text her. That way the text would lie in her phone, unseen until her day began tomorrow, or it could evoke my need and invite her to call me if she were wakeful enough.

I typed into my phone, "Hyacinth, Tanya is out of danger now. They will send her home as soon as she tests negative for contagion. Can you make a break with Seaways and come here to join me in raising your grandchildren?"

I didn't want to open up about Constance's removal as I was convinced it was temporary, especially now that my job was in jeopardy, and enforced absence from work had shown me that it barely covered the transport costs I paid to do it.

Hyacinth texted back, "Of course."

I sat on the freshly tidied bed, disentangling jewellery and hanging it on all the stands and frames Tanya had accumulated since we had lived in Southshire.

Then, before I was fully asleep in my own room, the mobile rang shrilly.

Hyacinth began abruptly, "I thought you would never ask."

"But, Hyacinth, you were the one who said I should move in here. It really only sleeps three."

"My first granddaughter is twenty-one," she reprimanded me. "Do you expect her to stay home forever? I'm sure we can squeeze until the Tanya bird takes her flight."

I giggled for the first time in days, "First right turn and straight on till morning," I quoted from my favourite children's book. "But she's written you a letter. Has she been talking to you about this?"

"Maybe, but if it's her letter to me, I'm sure she'll talk to me about it herself," Hyacinth laid down an order of privacy for us all before saying, "I have been sifting through solutions for you for several days now, I made this call for us to discuss them."

"Did you know I am charged with several offences?" I decided to come clean since she was worried enough to break her customary phone economy.

"I know; that's why I've been thinking of you. You can't come to a small town like this and expect to keep secrets," she affirmed.

"They said my work caused me to neglect Constance."

"Yes, and it could be true for, if your schedule said jump, you had to jump. It wasn't a question of being late for a call. How late can you be for a half-hour slot? If you are late, you've missed it altogether."

"So, they've put her in care."

"They haven't made a final decision. They've offered you help to get through a bad time."

Her reconstruction gave me hope because it made the care order reversible.

"When I move in, they will lose this argument against you," Hyacinth assured me.

"They say Tanya isn't qualified to give childcare. She needs training, they said."

"Let them try to say that of me," Hyacinth warned. "I am sure that, at my age, I have more skill and experience with children than most people alive."

"If you move in, will they say the flat is over-occupied?" I asked.

"Will you stop picking holes? I cannot come as a visitor to your home, so it will have to become my home. They cannot put me on the street if I terminate my contract here and relocate to my family."

"I may not have a job after next Monday," I informed her.

"That's fine," she said. "It's about time you set up your own business and stopped being a wage earner."

"I've never had a thought of business in my head!" I resisted.

"Well, now I've put it there!" my mother-in-law was triumphant. "You can start thinking of what you want to do."

"Hortense is bringing Darfield back into town!" I revealed in horror.

"Where he will be as subject to the gossip on the grapevine as you are! I don't think so. Even if she would want it, he wouldn't. Look at this, you haven't spoken his name since before Constance was born; now, you have obviously realised the close connection between Darfield and Hortense. Why is this making you panic?"

"But you knew the connection all along because I haven't explained it to you, and you've taken it on board as soon as I mentioned him."

"Yes, I know the danger of Darfield. He is Hortense's nephew. He did follow her to this town after he lost you as his lean-on-total-support, but he's greedy. There is not enough potential for him here. He has moved out to greener pastures, and he has nothing to gain from moving back. You will always flag him up if he crosses your path. This will not support his financial capacity to grasp fluid gain quickly and to put nothing back. You may not be the only woman who called him out, but he needs you to be the only one here so that you can be cowed, silenced, and unable to share. He may, make no mistake, dig a little harder for a little longer, but I'm watching him. So are you. So is Hortense. Teach Tanya your security system and get her to practice it too."

I was listening, breathless, to the far-reaching implications she drew from a man's loss of women's trust. She made me feel that women could form unbreakable alliances. Our mutual support could form a chain-link fence, providing resistance against those who saw an advantage in a long vista of future manipulations.

"So, I must teach Tanya to talk up like I do? Then, how has she written you a long deep letter about matters she has never shared with me? Is it possible to raise girls who are lionesses when you have had to be the head of the pride yourself?"

"Well, lions do," she assured me. "And this letter. You are very anxious for Tanya to share it with me. As soon as she is out of the hospital, she will. I look forward to it. Now, I have delayed your morning for long enough. Get on with life, girl. I'm sure you have things to do before your daughters come home."

The phone banged down. I shook my head at her spirit and glanced around my perfectly prepared home, hesitating about the time before going back to yesterday's turning point, at the edge of the cemetery. I was taken aback to see 4 am. I checked a clock as well as my phone and then submitted. Dawn came early in summer. Ward rounds started at 7. I could locate the boy, divest my family of Hortense's nephew, and get back to wait, with undivided attention to reuniting with each of my children in turn.

Chapter Fifteen
Tanya

I grabbed the prepacked bag, hesitated before putting it over my shoulder, then, nodding to myself, slipped a recent picture of Tanya into the bag.

Self-locking the front door, I put the key back under the stone, turned out towards the hills, and texted Hyacinth as I went. "Key under the stone right of the doorstep."

She's texting now, I thought, so she will see it. She's joined us in the Wi-Fi era at last.

On autopilot, I reached the cemetery corner. I turned upward under the trailing trees. I had not brought my stick, so I pulled up my hood to stop low twigs from tangling my hair. Up through the trees, I hesitated and started to tack right and left from the path, using all my senses to track a human presence.

I smelt for wood fires, listened, motionless, for crackling twigs, searched beneath branches and above undergrowth for changes of colour. Deep in the dappled morning distance, I saw a strong blue between the boles. *Too early for such a bright sky*, I thought, *too near to be the sea*.

I trod carefully towards it, cautious of disturbing the occupant, which I grew more and more certain to be the boy.

Now, countable strides away, I saw a fallen sapling, raised a few feet above the ground, with a blue tarpaulin stretched across it. I drew near with as few crackles as possible.

Out came the mac; I spread it, sat on it, and arranged the flask and food upon it.

I stretched my hand to touch a brown, roughened toe that protruded from the lowest edge of the tarpaulin.

A stifled cry and the caught corners of the tarpaulin strained and popped as the boy sat up and elbowed it from his face, fists in his eyes.

With a burst of his own language, he clearly asked me what on earth I was doing.

"You what?" I queried equally unintelligibly. I reached into the almost empty bag. I drew out Tanya's picture. I held it steadily for him to look at. I pointed to myself. "Mother, Mummy," I pronounced clearly. I cradled the hand that held the photo in my free arm to demonstrate my meaning.

Carefully using an international gesture of thanks, I rolled up onto my knees, clasped hands prayer-like, and bowed my head to him. He watched wide-eyed. His face opened in a sunny smile.

He pointed back at the picture and cradled his arms in agreement.

I stood up, pointed to the picture yet again, to myself, and back to the image of Tanya. I stepped aside and indicated the food and drink spread on the mat. He shuffled across from the fallen tarpaulin and tore into the food. I placed the binoculars beside him, bowed again, hands clasped, waved, put Tanya's picture in my pocket, and crashed, heedlessly away, over the undergrowth, beneath the trees, the hoodie tearing off in my haste, and my hair collecting leaves and seeds as low-hanging branches combed it.

Approaching the flat, I looked at my phone to see that two hours had passed. A taxi swept up behind me, and I assumed it was the regular one that collected the person who lived above me for work each day. I was wrong. The driver got out and opened the rear door ceremoniously before going around to the boot and lifting out suitcases and boxes. Hyacinth slowly unfolded herself from the back seat and gratefully grasped my outstretched hand. She leant on it stiffly for her first few steps through the gate but loosened and straightened as she followed the path to the front door.

She was surprised when I bent to take the key from under the stone. "Weren't you waiting for me?" she asked.

"Didn't you read my text message?" I responded.

"That's only for emergencies," she said.

I ushered her in and told myself about learning curves and how sensitive it would be to negotiate a three-generational household.

"What time is Constance due?" she asked. I did not know. I would have to check with Paul.

I tried to avoid too many references to the lawyer she had linked me with, but I did express gratitude for his help.

"That's what families do for each other," Hyacinth asserted. Then she added, "Let me speak to him too, please, when you get him," Hyacinth was settling onto the settee while I collected her luggage and arranged it along the wall in Constance's room. Dolls looked down in close concentration as I quickly calculated how the bags and boxes could be unpacked.

"Have you had breakfast?" I asked.

"Have you?" she asked.

We laughed, admitted the oversight, put the kettle on, and prepared cups, plates, and toast together.

The last dregs and crumbs were still around us when Hyacinth glanced at her wristwatch and said, "Paul."

I nodded, pulled out my phone, and clicked on his name.

"Good morning, Miss Roberts," Paul had not been taken by surprise. "Constance's foster parents have said they will be with you at 10 am. This is not a guarantee of access rights to come. That issue must go back to court."

I thought he was canvassing for more work and higher fees, so I spoke no further. I passed the phone to Hyacinth and heard her informing Paul that she had moved in, so the presence of a resident grandmother must be evidenced in his application to restore my custody rights.

Practical arrangements lessen stress. I told myself.

I wandered back to Constance's room. "I think you have to move," I addressed the dumb-founded toys, and, reaching up and gathering them into my arms, I trailed them upstairs and ranged them watchful along the tops of Tanya's wardrobes. Next, I fetched Constance's clothes and laid them on Tanya's bed, leaving the downstairs' wardrobe doors open for Hyacinth and then hanging her clothes. I invited her to finish this before I went back up and moved, shuffled, and rehung everything to accommodate both daughters in the same mezzanine space.

An hour still remained before Constance's arrival. I pulled out a tablet and clicked onto a swap site, making bids to exchange Tanya's bed for a bunk bed so that there would still be enough floor space upstairs.

I sourced fresh bed linen and a spare duvet from my own room and remade the downstairs bed while Hyacinth continued sorting her clothes.

10am approached. I took Constance's bed linen upstairs, folded it on Tanya's bed, and heard Constance's lively shout through the mezzanine window.

"Mummy," her eager shout changed to "Grandma!" as she caught sight of Hyacinth and was cuddled into her arms by the time, I stepped off the stairs. I went, composed and confident, to the front garden to meet the temporary foster parents. I saw a man, hesitant and scrawny, and a woman, sleek and confident. Her extended hand was cool and brief, dated by lockdown but followed by a quick, apologetic step back. "Call me Sharon," she said. "This is my partner, Alan."

Alan twitched and shuffled. I indicated the garden chairs alongside the front door. I did not invite them to sit, just assumed they would accept outdoor accommodation. I turned my attention to Constance, who was in awe of my changes, proud of her elevation to upstairs living, and overjoyed to find that her Grandma was a permanent addition to the family circle. After checking that she had eaten, I showed her the pictures I had received of bunk beds and asked her to choose which one she wanted to share with Tanya.

"But, Mummy, I need to talk to Tanya about that," she said.

"You soon will," I replied, joyfully, as I heard a heavy vehicle draw up outside. I hurried to greet Tanya from the ambulance and to help her, weakened but cool-skinned, up the path. I ignored the foster parents' inquiring stare and took Tanya inside to lie on the settee. Constance sat on the floor beside her, immediately showing her the tablet and asking her which bunk bed she preferred.

Tanya divided her attention between her sister and her Grandma as she watched Hyacinth, tactfully leaving the siblings undisturbed while she packed away her clothes.

Summing up the situation from the kitchen, I was reassured and replete to see a mornings' gathering that previewed the unity and security to come.

Chapter Sixteen
Lights

Now, I went to meet the foster crew.

"Sharon and Alan, did you say?" I asked.

They seemed reassured that I had remembered their names. "The lawyer said a decision will be taken in court tomorrow," I said. "Will you be there?"

They muttered something about Zoom.

"Yes, of course," I agreed to their inarticulate response. "Everything is online nowadays. I will be submitting video evidence." I don't know why I told them that, but the fearless assertion lay between us as a barrier to their continued income from the emergency care of my child.

The scrawny man shuffled his feet.

"Can you give him a hot drink?" Sharon asked. He's diabetic.

I was sorry she felt she had to expose his privacy in this way. I apologised for my lapse in hospitality and gained confidence from my ability to accept a failing without feeling challenged. I made Tanya a hot drink, as well, and went to sit at the foot of the settee while she drank it.

"What do you remember about the night before you were taken to the hospital?" I asked as Constance moved off to show Hyacinth the bed they had chosen.

Tanya wrinkled her nose in an effort to remember, "Lights," she said, "Green lights out at sea. Like the winking blue and red one's blinking back and forth from Hyacinth's window but bobbing closer and closer to shore."

"Do you remember climbing into a boat?" I asked.

"No, I watched the light bobbing nearer. I felt increasingly hot, as if it was bringing the heat. I was tired. I sat on the sand and watched it come nearer."

I lived in her skin and watched as my friendly boy beached his boat beside her drowsy figure and decided to secure her in it whilst he went to the town in search of food. He beached the boat, lodged it safe from the rising tide behind a boulder, and folded her into it. I imagined him checking her breathing and covering her with a blanket and a blue tarpaulin while he set out for an early morning forage in town. He would have expected to rouse her later and retrieve the boat for his return to the platform and his colleagues there.

Tanya was drowsy again. I stopped the prompting and the pondering and went back to the foster care people to gather ammunition against their continuation in the role.

"So, what drew you to this work?" I queried.

"We stay home," Sharon explained. "Alan's condition makes it hard for him to work. I have to monitor his blood sugars to safeguard him against hypoglycaemia and hyperglycaemia. Fostering gives us a chance to give something back to the society in return for what we get out."

My cold intention to extract evidence against their further involvement in my custody case became less judgmental. "Is the uncertainty of the condition the reason why you choose to take temporary cases?" I asked.

"Yes, we refuse cases when he is in crisis," Sharon acknowledged.

"Thank you for stepping in. We were going through some changes," I said.

"Well, you seem to be pretty well settled now." She had worked her way to the open door and was looking around a bit too observantly for my privacy.

"I'll bring you some sandwiches," I said. "You may need to check your partner's blood sugar while I make them for you."

This had the effect of making her withdraw. I ignored them, instead I made jam butties and ham sandwiches for her to select whichever she needed.

"Mummy, she has a gadget that lights up!" Constance said, having gone outside for a curious peep while Tanya was resting.

"I know; take these to them." I gave her the plate and hovered behind her to ask, "What is your schedule? Were you given a specific visit time for Constance this morning?"

"It's not too strict, but we need to be back by mid-day," Sharon replied.

"Will you be in the Zoom for her custody hearing?" I dared to ask.

"Yes, and we will put in a good word for you." She gave me a sudden smile.

"Can I let Constance bring some of her toys?" I asked.

"No," answered Sharon, "that wouldn't be fair on her. She'd have to leave them with us, and we'd have to bin them because of Covid regulations."

"I see," I said, my attitude to them hardening again but, careful not to lose my advantage, I jollied Constance along to the end of the call and told her we would send pictures and messages to Sharon's WhatsApp for her. Sharon unbent long enough to give me her contact number to use for the purpose and we parted amicably with Constance treating the day as an adventure and promising to be back with her Tanya, Grandma, and Mummy by the next day.

Moods were changed by flashing blue lights outside and the intrusion of both uniformed and plain-clothed police into my garden.

"But you said I would get the whole of this day to myself."

"We had leads," they said. "We want to clear up the case."

With more confidence than ever before, I said a brief farewell to Hyacinth and Tanya, reached for Darfield's picture and name tag under the clock, slipped them into my pocket, and left with the officers.

In the interview room, they raised the issue of the boat again. After beating around the bush, they said they had made a discovery in the woods that morning and asked if I knew about a boy who was hiding out up there.

"Yes," I said. "I visited him this morning."

"We know you did," my favourite officer agreed. She wore a green suit set this morning. "We followed you."

I swallowed hard. I had, in effect, given him up to the authorities. "What will you do with him?" I asked.

"We'll take him into care and treat him as a vulnerable minor while his papers are examined and sorted." I hoped he would be placed with Sharon and Alan. "You needn't worry about him," she added gently, "He is covered by the Human Rights Act and Safeguarding of Minors policies."

I nodded and drew the name tag and pictures from my pocket. "This is the man who owns the boat," I said. "His full name is Darfield. I was married to him briefly once."

"You had his child." I ignored her irrelevance. But responded to her next query. "Who is the woman in the picture?"

I told her she was Hortense, and she was his aunt. The Officer nodded to the uniformed person behind me, who left the room. "Your client at Seaways. The person who invited your mother-in-law to our town and set wheels in motion for you to reside here."

She smiled gently now as if she apologised for the whole mistaken drift of their investigations to this point. She carefully put the name tag and the photo into a zip-lock bag and handed it to the officer when he returned. "How long?" she asked.

"Ten to fifteen minutes," he said and left again.

My green-clad lady leaned forward and switched off the camcorder, an object I had ceased to notice; I was so used to it.

"Mrs Roberts, thank you for assisting us with our inquiries," she said graciously as if my co-operation had been by choice. Automatically rejecting the unspoken apology, I pointed out that the camcorder was off and asked her to turn it on, repeat her thanks and add a statement of her belief in my innocence. She did as I asked so far as she was legally able, and the camcorder winked twice to acknowledge her switch on and switch off.

I stood, shook myself, and made for the door. "You will take care of that boy, won't you?" I spoke. "My daughter could have died of Covid out there if he hadn't sheltered her. It cost him his boat and his independence."

"Maybe, but he gained your protection from Darfield, and often, our job is to follow up the small fry until they lead us to the big fish. You will be called upon to testify," she said.

"I'll talk to my lawyer to make it a part of my plea bargain," I warned.

"You are released without charge," she assured me.

"What happened to driving with inadequate eyesight?" I challenged, "That will cost me my job."

"It doesn't pay much. Start a business," she echoed Hyacinth as she hustled me out, almost bumping into Hortense in the corridor.

My ex-client turned up her aquiline nose.

I had once enjoyed my simple, loving employment. If my assumptions about the integrity of life in our little town could not be repaired, I would have to think again. I was no longer an innocent caregiver. I had seen the dark underbelly of this sedate life in Southshire.

I went out into the fresh air, thinking of coloured lights, refracting lenses, and closed candle shops.

Maybe, out of this would come my business idea.

The End

Lights at Sea is Palmer's second novel. The first emerged from many years of residence in Jamaica and a close friendship with Eva Jones, the Archivist of our town. She wanted to recount the stories of her life, but asked me to scramble them through history. Out of her recollections, each of my heroines was born. Knitting them together with Amy's story is a tribute to my friend. Eva Jones passed away just as the book was about to be published.

Hues of Blackness: A Jamaican Saga was published by Strategic Books and is available from Amazon.

Forthcoming is its sequel that looks at men's experience, provisionally titled *Coastal Turf*.

Miranda's story continues in *The Candle Shop*. Southshire is a fictionally contracted area relating to Kent and Sussex together and extending along the coast to include Bournemouth. *The Candle Shop* leads to the family's travels to their other origins in Jamaica.